After All

Janice R. Johnson

FpS

Greenville, S.C.

After All
by Janice R. Johnson

Copyright © 2023 Janice R. Johnson

Published by:

FpS

1175 Woods Crossing Rd., #2
Greenville, S.C. 29607
864-675-0540
www.fiction-addiction.com

ISBN: 978-1-952248-97-9

Cover art by the author's granddaughter, Leira Johnson. Special thanks to the author's grandson Jay Israel and to Chelsea Marks for posing for the cover art.

Cover & Book Design by Vally Sharpe of United Writers Press.

Printed in the United States of America

After all…

Dedicated to
John William Johnson

For our life's journey, filled with
love, laughter, faith, family, patience, team,
dedication, understanding, encouragement, and hope.

May 1967

Tears welled up in Jessica Reynolds's eyes as she stood in the line of bridesmaids watching Claire join Tom at the altar. She had imagined so many times standing with Carter Powell at a church altar as they pledged their forever love to each other.

It had been almost nine months since Carter's death in Vietnam. Dealing with his loss had been painful and had created a vacuum in her heart. Her thoughts flashed back to his last letter to her—his wish for her to find joy despite his being gone and to love again. The counseling she had received since that day echoed Carter's words—encouraging her to move on.

The crescendo of the organ proclaiming that Tom and Claire were now officially husband and wife brought her back to the present. She straightened her shoulders and prepared to follow the new married couple down the aisle. She glanced at the many faces of those gathered— who, during her deepest grief, had stood by her side.

Chapter 1

October 1966

S hots from the 21-gun salute rang in Jessie Reynolds's ears. Standing by the grave, she held a single red rose from the arrangement her parents had sent to the church that morning. Like their daughter, Madeline and Ladd Reynolds loved Carter Powell and had envisioned his joining their family.

Jessie watched the 1965 Northwest High teammates, one by one, say their goodbyes as they passed Carter's grave. When she saw Coach Paul O'Connor at the end of line, she pulled the purple shawl he had placed around her shoulders at the church closer and felt its warmth.

Jack Mason stood waiting to walk her to his car. For years, he had been the one who had always been there, bringing fun and laughter to their friendship. They had grown up together from elementary school and had shared classes throughout their years at Northwest. Their friendship had continued when they'd both gone to the University of Georgia—and he had been a rock for Jessie from the moment she had received the news about Carter.

"I can bring you back later, if you like, Jess," said Jack. "Maybe after everyone has left?" Jessie nodded and took his arm to leave the cemetery hillside.

Her parents followed them to the car. "Honey, we need to get you something to eat," said Madeline. Jessie had no appetite, but she knew her mother was right.

Jack opened the passenger door of his Volkswagen and she climbed into the car. As they pulled away, she stared out the window through the tall pines surrounding the cemetery and watched as the October sun sank below the horizon. Numb and still in denial, she looked up into the clouds and felt empty.

Coach O'Connor watched as they disappeared through the cemetery gates and returned to the graveside to join Carter's brother Bobby and his fiancée, Marie. As Carter's closest living relative, Bobby had been given the American flag, folded with precision by the military escort. He held the flag close to his chest with one hand and extended the other to the coach. "This day has been painful, but I am so proud of Carter," he said. "He's with Papa Ford now. I'll bet they're sharing their war stories." A lone tear ran down his cheek.

Coach O'Connor thought of the young man he had privately claimed as a son. He hoped Carter would share those same stories with his wife Ann, who had died four years before. He was sure she was pleased that he had given her purple shawl to Jessie.

Rev. Stephen Hamilton joined them and stood in silence. He knew the days ahead would be tough for them all —himself included. He'd committed to James Crawford before his death to care for and minister to his grandsons. The tragic car accident that had taken the boys' parents had left few family members behind to care for them since their grandfather's death. The minister had been the primary resource to Bobby in caring for his best interests as well as his younger brother's. Bobby thanked the pastor for officiating the service and then turned away to take Marie's arm and walk toward their car, leaving the coach and minister at the graveside alone. "You know, Stephen," said the coach to his friend and confidant. "Carter knew all along that his real father was Martin Garrett."

Hamilton shook his head. "In all our conversations over the years, Carter never shared his awareness of that information with me," he said. He placed a hand on the coach's shoulder. "I don't think Carter ever thought of Garrett as his 'real' father, Paul. He had a fine father figure in you. Don't forget that."

A sad smile appeared on the coach's face. "I only hope he knew how much I cared."

JACK WALKED JESSIE TO THE FRONT of the Reynolds' home and waited as she walked through the door. Although it had been days since she'd received the news, she continued to show no signs of emotion. The hollow look in her eyes said it all—she was still in shock.

Madeline Reynolds stood at the door. "Jack, won't you come in and have some dinner with us?"

"Thank you, Mrs. Reynolds, but I think maybe Jessie needs some time with just the two of you." Jack's feelings for Jessie had not wavered—and he wanted only what was best for her. When he reached his car, he turned to see Jessie's father, Ladd, holding her in his arms.

It had been an emotional day. As Jack drove toward home, he thought of the day in the park when he encountered Carter after he had told Jessie he was headed to Vietnam. "Take care of her for me, Jack," he had said, unaware of the feelings he'd had for Jessie long before Carter had come into her life. Jack shifted his thoughts to going back to college in Athens.

It was the middle of a semester, and he knew Jessie would have to soon face the thought of returning herself.

"Come to the kitchen with me," said Madeline to her daughter. "Let's see what you might like to eat. Maybe some scrambled eggs or some of the soup that Mrs. Crosby brought by this morning?"

The Reynolds' close neighbors were all aware of Carter's death—and Jessie's relationship with him. After an article about his being killed in Vietnam had appeared in the *Atlanta Journal*, American flags had appeared up and down Longwood Drive.

"I really want to lay down," said Jessie finally. "I'm tired." She tried to offer a grateful smile to her parents. "I'll come back down later."

All that had happened in the past few days had exhausted her. Communicating with all the well-intentioned people who had attended the funeral had sapped all her energy. Jessie wanted only the haven her room had always been to her.

As she climbed the steps, she remembered a night she had been sick, and Carter had carried her up to her bedroom. By the time she reached the top of the stairs, the grief finally overcame her. With Ann O'Connor's purple shawl still wrapped tightly around her, she opened the door and crossed the room to her bed. When her head touched her pillow, she pulled the blanket Carter had given her the past Christmas over her and, stroking it softly, allowed the tears she had held too long inside to flow.

Madeline sat at the kitchen table with her husband. "Ladd, whatever can we do for her?"

"I don't know. Just be here for her?" he said. "It is going to take some time. Rev. Hamilton said he is here to help."

"Going back to school right now may not be the best for her," said Madeline. "She's so fragile. Jack has offered to take her back to school and watch out for her."

"Yes, but we can't take advantage of him. It wouldn't be fair."

JACK STEPPED THROUGH THE GARAGE DOOR of his parents' house and pulled off his tie. His mother turned from the kitchen sink and smiled. "Hey, honey. How's Jessie?"

He shrugged his shoulders. "I wish I knew," he said.

As a child, Jack Mason had never asked for much. His parents, who, with his aunt and uncle, ran a small Atlanta restaurant and grill near Georgia Tech, had raised a son with a warmhearted spirit and genuine kindness to all those who knew him. Through the years, the family's one-story ranch home had been a place of hospitality and welcome to his friends. They had grown up knowing there was always a place for them at the Mason's table. There was even a cooler in the garage with soft drinks for the taking.

Jack's aunt and uncle, with no children of their own, had also helped to raise him—adding their contributions to instilling in him a love of life, laughter, and family. He had learned from them all about the family business and had worked weekends and summers at the grill. He'd often joined his aunt and uncle on trips to their cabin on the lake near Clayton. The cabin was not far from Athens—he could drive over for swimming and fishing and as needed to help with repairs and maintenance.

Jack's parents' home was across Howell Mill, not far from where the Reynolds lived. For years he and Jessie had shared the same schools and neighborhood friendships. He had often joined the Baldwin brothers and other friends for pickup football games at Memorial Park, where he'd first encountered Carter Powell. They become good friends when they played together on the Northwest High football team.

During his senior year, the Northwest yearbook staff had named

Jack one of the twelve senior superlatives and he had been chosen "Most Friendly" by his classmates. It was an award of distinction among all the Northwest seniors. Coach O'Connor had recognized him at the annual Sports Banquet with a special Senior Leader award. Whether greeting everyone at the Buckhead Zesto hangout or with smiles in the school hallway, Jack was as dependable as they come. He was accepted by all his classmates knowing they could count on his friendship and good intentions.

Although a wiry kid during his adolescence, in the last few years at Northwest his workouts with the football team were reflected in his physique, and girls who hadn't taken him seriously began to take new notice. He had gone from being the class fun-loving guy to a steady, dependable friend—traits any girl would appreciate in a match. But he couldn't have the one person—the one girl—whose attention he wanted most. His friend Carter had stepped in and taken her away.

Jack's UGA freshman year had begun well. He had arrived in Athens and met his roommate, Davis Whitlock, from Villa Rica. It hadn't taken long for Jack to realize that Davis was more there to enjoy his college freedom than for higher learning.

The two got along well, but most often went their separate ways when it came to socializing. Davis hung out with the small-town rowdies who had joined him in making the leap to the larger campus life. Jack came back to their room in Payne Hall more often than he liked to find leftover food and beverage containers scattered across the floor. Strict rules existed prohibiting students from having alcohol in campus dorms, but Davis seemed unconcerned.

But Jack's outgoing personality put him high on several fraternity bid lists, and he pledged Pi Kappa Phi. The brothers on Milledge Avenue felt like a perfect fit.

He had packed hurriedly when Jessie's dad had called him about the news of Carter's death. His only thought had been to go to Jessie's side. The funeral over, he now needed to return to Athens, but he already knew that Jessie would not be going back with him. He had spoken to Rev. Hamilton after the funeral about it.

"She knows you are there for her, Jack," the minister had said.

"I hope so," Jack had told him. "I know in my head that she needs time."

He stepped around his mother and kissed her on the cheek. "I'm going to pack. I'm going back to Athens tomorrow," he said.

"Okay, son," she said. "Your dad is bringing home some food from Mason's to take back with you." She watched as he turned and went down the hallway. Although he'd never told her as much, she had long known how he felt about Jessie Reynolds.

REV. HAMILTON RETURNED TO THE CHURCH to complete his notes and thoughts for the Sunday service. His calling to ministry at the Sandy Springs Methodist church was still strong although it had been the young minister's first assignment fresh out of seminary. The congregation had grown significantly since the year of his installation—the larger local community depended on him as well. It was early in his ministry that Coach Paul O'Connor had recruited him to be the Northwest High football team's chaplain and he'd been introduced to Frank Caldwell, the team's physician. A regular round of golf with the two of them gave him relished moments of "time out" from being on call 24/7—the sermons, weddings, funerals, hospital visitations, church meetings, and calls in the middle of the night which gave him little opportunity to re-energize himself.

He walked into the sanctuary and headed down a side aisle toward his office and glanced around at the light of the sun still streaming through the stained-glass windows. The theme of the Crawford Memorial window, "Inviting Christ," had always been a reminder to him to lay down his burdens and pick up the renewal of a new day. He stopped at the window and took a deep breath before continuing to his office—a ritual established long before when he'd agreed to watch over the two Powell brothers after their Grandfather Crawford's death.

Now there was only one.

Coach O'Connor unlocked the front door of his Garden Hills cottage and turned on the light. The day had been an emotional one, a reminder of many memories. He stopped at his late wife Ann's floral chair in the living room. Until today, the arm had always been covered by a beautiful purple shawl with a silver thread of hope that she had woven years before. He'd felt strongly that Ann had guided him to give the shawl to Jessie. Was this a sign to him from his precious wife that, after four years, it was time for him to move on?

More than ever, his thoughts turned to what more there could be. He had no idea where to even begin—he had been unable to even consider it before now. But the events of recent days had cruelly reminded him once again that, no matter what, "Life is short," and our job is to make the most of every day.

Stephen Hamilton had counseled him after Ann's death about all he offered to those around him. Not just the students of Northwest and the players on his team. Not just in the care for his garden. "You have much to offer to a more personal relationship, too," Stephen had said, "And I don't mean with your golfing buddies." With Stephen's encouragement, Coach O'Connor had written down thoughts about the future. His focus and morning meditation began on the front porch each day with his departed Ann and his garden as inspiration. He made notes in a small notebook kept on his desk—a gentle reminder to him of the preciousness of life.

Now he'd suffered yet another loss. Although Carter had not been his biological child, he had allowed himself to feel the joy of a father-son connection with him.

He picked up the notebook and opened the front cover. Carter's last note to him was tucked inside. He flipped through the book, reading his scribbled thoughts and images. In the margin of one page was the word "Egleston"—a reminder of Ann and his volunteer time and commitment to the children at the Egleston Children's Hospital.

He leaned back in his chair and thought. That was where he would begin. During the upcoming holiday season, he would plan a trip to the children's hospital near Emory University. He took a deep breath and slowly released it. He was ready to discover the *more* life offered …and what he had to offer it.

Chapter 2

Sergeant Matthew Randall knocked on the frame of the open office door at Fort Benning. Lieutenant Thacker looked up from the stack of reports piled on his desk. "Yes, what is it, Randall?" he said.

The young sergeant stood at attention. "Sir. Yes, sir. Have you had any word about our next assignment?"

The lieutenant shook his head. "At ease. No, no word yet. It could be months before we get our new orders. What's on your mind?"

Matt relaxed his stance. "I spoke with the chaplain this morning, sir. I asked him for some family information on our men…you know, the ones we lost."

"What kind of information?"

"Family and loved ones, sir. My R&R isn't scheduled yet. I have some time, and while I waited, I thought I might write to some of them and offer my personal condolences."

Thacker gazed up at the young man, not too much younger than he, and looked back at the papers on his desk.

"It is a worthy idea, Randall, but I must warn you of the consequences."

"Consequences, sir?"

"Your experiences with your men. Watching them die. Some in your arms. Your own feelings will be matched, even exceeded, by the pain and grief of their loved ones. Contacting them can tear you apart just as much, even more." He paused. "But…it can be a gift to them too. Closure they may be searching for."

Matt saluted his boss and turned to leave. "Yes, sir," he said quietly.

Sergeant Matthew Chapman Randall had come from a long line of military officers. He and his mother and sister had followed his father from base to base in his early years. When asked where he was "from," Matt had always struggled to answer. He had no real roots—there had been no time to establish lasting friendships or relationships, especially when he knew he could be gone again tomorrow. Aside from family, his primary relationship had been with his fellow soldiers.

The military life hadn't taken a toll only on Matt, however. After years of marital strife, his parents had gone their separate ways. Matt had lived during the school years with his mother and sister and in the summers with his father. His mother had instilled in him a sense of compassion for others, while his father, a man of often harsh words, had ingrained in him a dedication to country, of what it meant to be a man. As a boy, Matt had had no other thought but to follow in his father's footsteps.

Matt had the option to reenlist, but after the result of his unit's bloody tour in Vietnam, if he remained in the service once his time in was done, he intuitively knew his emotional survival depended on his taking care of himself. He had avoided saying anything like that to his commanding officers but had sought out the chaplain. Their conversations had strengthened his resolve while offering the solace of a safe mentor and a religious foundation he had never known. The chaplain had suggested that Matt take a trip away from the base. "It might give you a chance to find some inner peace," he said.

This had made Matt think of the farm his mother's family owned near Cross Hill, South Carolina. His mom had spent her childhood summers there and had often taken Matt and his sister back for visits. The farmhouse had been kept in repair by "Mr. Roy." There were plenty of things for kids to do—fishing, hunting, swimming in the lake, horseback riding and picking fresh vegetables from the garden.

He smiled to himself. A trip to the farm might be just what he needed. Plus, there, he'd have the time and quiet to write the families of the young men in his platoon. It would be hard not to be with family for Thanksgiving, but Christmas would be only a few weeks after. He wondered if his parents could co-exist for a few days without the awkwardness of years past. His father would have to travel from Puerto Rico, where he'd retired, and his mother and sister from their home on the North Carolina coast outside of Wilmington.

On his way back from Lt. Thacker's office, he stopped by to see the chaplain again. "Sir, is it still possible to get those names and addresses?"

The chaplain nodded and handed him a typed list of the addresses of the men in his unit. Matt glanced down at the sheets. "I went to see Lt. Thacker this morning and he told me to be careful. I wouldn't want to invade their privacy or cause any more heartache."

The chaplain smiled. "I feel sure the families of your men will appreciate any personal words about their loved ones."

Like his father, Matt was not a man of many words. But like his mother, he was a man of compassion and he hoped the right ones would come when he finally sat down to write.

Chapter 3

Perry Michaels had returned from visiting relatives for Thanksgiving and was bent over folders on his desk. The office door opened and he looked up to see his assistant. "Hi, Courtney, how was your holiday?"

"Ate too much as usual, but it was good to see my parents." She paused. "Did you hear the news about Carter Powell—you know, the drummer for the Playboys?"

"No, what?"

"He was killed in Vietnam. A contact at one of the local clubs called me. She saw it in the *Atlanta Journal*."

Perry shook his head. "Wow. I was just looking at some of the responses we've gotten about the song he sent me before he left. They're actually quite positive."

The Playboys' southeastern summer tour bookings that Perry's agency had handled had gone well. There were high hopes for the band going forward, but all their plans had fallen apart when Carter announced he had enlisted in the Army. When he left for basic training, the group had broken up—the other members had gone their separate ways.

"What are you going to do about the song?"

"I guess we'll keep going," said Perry. "When Carter sent the lyrics, he went so far as to tell me what to do with any royalties if something happened to him." He pulled a folder from the stack and shuffled the papers. "Here it is. If any money is made from the song, the proceeds should go to his girlfriend, Jessie Reynolds. He wrote the song for her." He looked up at his assistant. "Do we know how to contact her?"

"I don't think so," said Courtney, thinking. "But you're still in touch with Crow Perkins, right? He'd know how to get in touch with her."

"Good idea," said Perry.

The phone rang on Crow's bedside table in the "Nest," the hangout in the basement of his parents' house. It was the place he had shared through the years with the members of the band he and Carter Powell had started in high school. When the Playboys had broken up, Crow, who had graduated from Clemson the previous June, had turned it into an apartment until he and Brandi, his longtime girlfriend and fiancée, were married. He reached for the phone. "Hello."

"Hi, Crow, this is Perry Michaels."

"Hey, Perry. What's up?"

"I just heard about Carter. I'm so sorry."

"Yeah, we're all shook up about it. He was like a brother to me." They continued to talk about Carter, the war and how too many young men were dying in Vietnam while protests were continuing to crop up across the country.

Perry sighed. "So, Crow, what do you think I should do about his song?"

"What song?"

The agent paused. "Oh, I thought you knew. Before Carter left for Vietnam, he sent me a letter and in it were the lyrics to a song called Hope: A Song for Jessie."

"You mean Jessie Reynolds. Wow! I didn't know anything about it."

"Well, he sent it to me and asked if I thought it had potential. Said if I thought it did, to seek some musical scoring to go with the words." He paused again. "Matter of fact, I think it's quite good. I have been working on it and making inquiries since he left, and the response has been very positive. It comes at a time when our country could use some hope."

"I had no idea. But now that you mention it, I do remember him scribbling in a notebook all the time when we were on the road. And you say it was dedicated to Jessie?"

"Yes. He said in his letter that if anything came of it, the royalties would go to her," said Perry. "I vaguely remember a young woman there with him for the band tour sendoff. If you are in touch with her, could you let her know to get in touch with me? I'll get back to you when I know more from my production contacts."

Crow sighed. "It's been almost a month since Brandi and I saw her at the funeral. I'm not sure how things are for her. I heard she didn't go back to college this semester. Carter and Jessie were very serious. More than a high school romance, you know."

"Like I said, no hurry. It could take some time unless the right person in the right place sees the lyrics and connects with it."

"Sure. Thanks for calling," said Crow. "I'll let Jessie know. And, please, keep me posted, too."

Chapter 4

"Merry Christmas, Jack," said the voice on the telephone.
His heart skipped a beat. "Jess, is that you?"

Since returning to UGA, Jack had picked up the telephone many times to call Jessie but had replaced the receiver, heeding Rev. Hamilton's advice. *She knows you are there for her.* "Merry Christmas! How are you, Jess?"

"I'm okay." Her tone seemed different from the last time he'd spoken to her. "I was thinking you would be home soon for the holidays. Am I calling at a bad time?"

"Oh, no. It's a good time. I finished my last exam this morning and am packing to head home."

"I'm hoping we can see each other while you're home."

Jack felt a tug in his heart. He too had struggled after Carter's death, and he was torn. He wanted to be there for Jessie in her grief, but he still had feelings for her himself. Her moving on after Carter would take time—the last thing he wanted was to pressure her into a relationship for all the wrong reasons.

"Maybe we could get together soon?" continued Jessie.

"How about tomorrow?" he said.

"Yes, and early! My mom asked if you could help us with something. Could you come over around five?"

Jack packed his Volkswagen and got ready to leave his Payne Hall dorm and head home. Highways out of Athens in all directions were filling with the exit of student vehicles for the holiday break. He kept an eye on his speedometer to make sure he didn't get a ticket in renewed excitement for his trip home to Atlanta.

SINCE THE FUNERAL, JESSIE HAD SPENT a lot of time with Rev. Hamilton. His counseling had helped her focus on gratitude for Carter. For his service to his country. For the love they had shared and for his words of encouragement to her in his final letter. The reverend had told her that reaching out to her longtime friends and not closing herself off to their support would be important in her recovery.

He'd been right. Jessie's parents had arranged for the rest of her belongings from the dorm to be packed and sent home to Atlanta after Carter's funeral, and the girls on her floor at Creswell Hall had made cards with messages of support for her. Although she had not been around them for long, her decision to go through sorority rush in September had been a good one—her Alpha Chi Omega sisters had sent cards and notes as well. Her initiation had been scheduled for spring, but it would be postponed if she didn't return for the spring semester. As the Christmas holidays had approached, she'd continued to struggle with when to return to school and how to re-enter her life without Carter.

She was sure that the holidays would help. Jessie's sisters, Caroline and Meredith, were coming home and would be there for church services, holiday mealtimes, and gifts. Her dad had brought out the boxes of decorations from the attic and her mother had given each family treasure its place of honor throughout the home. Ladd added colorful strands of lights around the front porch railings along with a fresh balsam wreath purchased at the state farmer's market. Behind each act of holiday love—from baking to decorating—was the thought of bringing some happiness back to the family after the enormous sadness they had all experienced in the fall.

PROMPTLY AT 5:00 P.M. THE NEXT evening, Jack rang the doorbell at the Reynolds home. Madeline opened the door and embraced him. "I am so happy to see you. Please come in."

Once inside, he looked around the living and dining rooms, noting the holiday decor so carefully placed. Vanilla and spice aromas from the kitchen brought an even larger smile to his face.

Mr. Reynolds appeared from the kitchen wiping his hands on a make-shift kitchen-towel "apron" tucked at his waist. "So good to see you, Jack. School going well?" He held up the edge of the towel and laughed. "Madeline's got me busy scooping oranges for her famous ambrosia. In fact, she's had me standing at the kitchen sink for most of the day. She keeps it refrigerated, ready to serve in her special crystal compotes."

Madeline pointed at Ladd. "You mean *your* famous ambrosia! With the holidays here, I can only imagine what's going on at Mason's about now."

Jack grinned. "It's good to see you both. And, yes, things are busy at Mason's. I'm sure I'll be helping out there while I'm home." He glanced around the room and looked for signs of Jessie.

"Jessie is downstairs in the rec room," said Madeline with a smile. She knew exactly who he wanted to see and that as a guest at the Reynolds' home many times, he knew exactly where to find the stairs in the kitchen leading down to the pine-paneled rec room below. She also suspected this young man was the healing medicine her daughter needed.

Jack turned at the bottom of the stairs to see Jessie, her back toward him, in front of a beautiful Frazier fir adorned with strings of white lights. Her hair was longer than it had been the last time he'd seen her. Strands of soft curls lay over her shoulders and the lights glowed around her. She turned toward him, and he felt instantly nervous, unsure of how she would receive him.

Jessie smiled and opened her arms. "Jack, I've missed you."

"Merry Christmas, Jess." He moved to hug her. "I've missed you, too." They held their embrace for a few short seconds and then stepped back to gaze at each other.

Jessie looked at Jack with what seemed new eyes. She wanted the afternoon to be more about the renewal of their already special bond than recalling the last time they'd been together. "I asked Mother if we could save the tree decorating for when you came home." She pointed to the boxes on the sofa.

Jack looked at Jessie and saw the girl he had known since their Brandon days, sat across from him in art classes and trips to the Zesto. He could remember his earliest thoughts of wishing for more than a friendship with her. And now he was sharing in the Reynolds family tradition.

"We have all kinds of ornaments we have collected over the years," she said, and handed him one. "Tell me about school."

Jack took the ornament and placed it up high. "Well, it has been interesting," he said. "My fraternity brothers have kept us pledges pretty busy," he said. "You know, trying to give us a hard time with all kinds of orders to earn our initiation." He chose not to mention the repeated efforts of the fraternity "sweetheart" to match him up with dates.

He picked up another ornament from one box, a delicate angel. "This one is pretty," he said, deciding not to acknowledge that it reminded him of her. It was way too early in their reunion for that, he thought.

She nodded. "That one goes way back. It was given to me by my grandmother. Here, let's add some garland too." As they worked, their conversation returned to a time of celebration—a celebration of special friends and kindred spirits.

Jack kept hearing the voice of Rev. Hamilton in his head. *Give her time.* "Campus was looking pretty quiet with everyone heading home for the holidays. Have you heard from Claire or Missy?"

"Yes. Missy has been good to keep me posted on activities there in Athens and Claire has been writing me from Duke. I want to see everyone," said Jessie. "I *need* to see everyone, I know."

"We'll do it together," Jack checked her reaction, "if that's okay with you."

"I'd like that. I know you have other plans and plenty of things to do…but I'd like that."

He smiled. "Good. Some of the gang are meeting out at the old Kennedy place on the river tomorrow night around seven. There will be a bonfire, but you better wrap up. The temperature will drop after dark."

Jessie handed Jack another ornament and felt a renewed energy with him at her side. "It will be good to see everyone."

In time off during the break from school, Paul O'Connor had reflected a lot, recording his thoughts in a small notebook. It had become clear in his mind that he needed a change. He was especially thankful for Stephen Hamilton. The reverend had been a rock of support and their friendship and counsel meant the world to him.

He woke early before his alarm and, with a cup of coffee, took a seat on the front steps of his Garden Hills cottage to watch the sunrise—a daily morning routine, regardless of the weather. Only rain ever caused him to pause under the covered front doorstep.

This morning felt different somehow. He gazed out over the garden. Since Ann's death, it had been his sanctuary. He'd begun each day focusing on the beauty of nature and the people and things in his life. Carter and Jessie had brought new hope…but having lost Carter, he searched for a renewed sense of purpose.

At the beginning of the holidays, Coach had made a trip to visit Egleston Children's Hospital. His late wife Ann had been a regular volunteer there and the hospital staff remained close to him. They saw a side of the coach that others seldom saw in his care, attention and play with the young children. Many children were medically fragile, unable to be as active as the talented athletic teens he coached at Northwest.

One of the staff who knew of his connection to Jessie told him she had visited the children too, entertaining them with her music and spending time in the art room sketching with them.

He sipped his coffee and felt its warmth. If the children only knew the gift of joy they always brought to him.

Chapter 5

Madeline reached in the mailbox for a stack of Christmas cards addressed to the family and made her way back in the house. A large basket on the coffee table held the many cards and notes they'd already received from family and friends. She shuffled through the envelopes and retrieved the brass letter opener kept on the mahogany secretary. "Jessie," she called out, "you have some mail."

Jessie joined her mother on the sofa. Madeline saw a new bounce in her daughter's step—ever since Jack's visit the day before Jessie's spirit had seemed to have changed. "Here, honey. This one's for you," said Madeline.

Jessie glanced at the envelope and her expression changed. She recognized the postmark and the special stamp from Columbus, Georgia she had seen before —on letters Carter had sent before his deployment to Vietnam.

"What is it, dear?"

Jessie slumped in her seat. "I don't know." She opened the letter and read the handwritten message.

Dear Miss Reynolds,

I received your name and address from our chaplain's office and I pray you are well.

My letter comes to you to say a word of gratitude for the bravery and courage of Private Carter Powell, who served in my platoon. It was my honor to be the officer who saw the heart and soul of a man who would do anything to represent his unit and country and had the trust of his fellow soldiers.

The men in our platoon spoke often of Private Powell's dedication and dependability in everything he did. He stepped up every time to accept any assignment needed for his unit and never once complained of any hardship. It was easy to tell he had the support of his family, loved ones and friends, which I don't state lightly. I carry to this day in my mind the phrase I saw written on his helmet – One Day at a Time. It will continue to be a way for those of us who know we must carry on and honor his words with our actions.

I want you to know that if there is ever anything I can say or do to bring you any sense of comfort in the days ahead, I am at your service. Having heard him speak of his family and you, I am confident he would have done the same for me. I pray that the words of this letter do not bring you any further pain but give you peace for your days ahead.

Respectfully,
Sgt. Matthew C. Randall

She sat for a moment, then handed the letter to her mother to read and stood. "I think I'll go for a walk."

The chill in the air was typical for the time of year in Atlanta, so Jessie reached for her coat in the hallway. As she made her way down Longwood, the wind picked up and she pulled her coat collar up to shield her neck.

Her mind flooded with memories as she made her way past the homes of the friends she'd known since childhood. The sun peeked through the December clouds and, when she saw the familiar shortcut next to the drainage grate halfway down the street, her step quickened. The path through the clearing down to the creek bed was the neighborhood access to Memorial Park—and the bank on Peachtree Creek she had shared with Carter. She had not returned to the spot since the day Carter had told her of his enlistment.

It had been some time since Jessie had left for her walk, and Madeline was concerned. As she reached for the front door, her daughter opened it. The expression on her daughter's face was different.

"Jessie? What is it?"

Jessie shook her head. "I can't explain it." She removed her coat and turned back toward her mother. "I went to the park," she said, "and I wish I could describe the feeling I had when I got there. I went to the spot Carter and I always spent time—the place where he told me he was enlisting." She paused. "I thought I'd be sad…especially after reading Sergeant Randall's letter."

"And were you?"

"No, I wasn't. But I can't really tell you why. At first, after I read the letter, I thought I wouldn't go with Jack to the bonfire tonight. But now

I really want to go. Strange...it's like this heaviness has been lifted."

Madeline wrapped an arm around her daughter and followed her to the den off the living room. "The letter was so nice. How thoughtful of the sergeant to write it."

Jessie's smile was bright. "Yes, it was." She took a seat on the bench at the piano in the den. Her eyes fell on a folder of sheet music she had taken with her to Egleston. Music had been her own therapy over the years—it brought her comfort as being with the children did.

"Will you be going out to Egleston again soon?" asked Madeline.

"I think so," said Jessie. "The children like to draw while I play the piano. I want to take them some special art supplies." She opened the piano bench to find a book with a medley of Christmas carols and turned its pages.

Madeline returned to the kitchen and listened as she heard the opening chords of "Joy to the World" and Jessie singing the words. With grateful tears in her eyes, she said a silent prayer for Jack's visit, the letter, and her daughter's recovery.

JACK ARRIVED AT SEVEN SHARP FOR their drive to the Chattahoochee. As they turned off Longwood, Jessie realized that had not seen many friends since the funeral and had missed their times together.

He flipped the car radio from station to station to find the right sound for their ride toward the densely wooded Riverside Drive. Jessie heard Jackie Wilson's "Whispers Getting Louder" play and the song caught her attention. She became so absorbed in the words that she realized Jack had been talking and had missed what he was saying. "I'm sorry. What did you say?" she asked.

"It's nothing," he said, glancing over at her. "Lost in thought?"

"I've never really listened to the words of that song," she said. Wilson sang the phrase again. *The whispers getting louder, calling your name.*

"What about them?" he asked.

"Just that…I don't know. It's something that…" Her voice trailed off. "Maybe we can talk about it later."

Jack parked on the upper street side near the abandoned driveway. The moonlit night was clear, which made their walk down the steep incline less treacherous. He'd intentionally avoided taking Jessie near places with special memories of Carter. He reached for her hand, and she grasped his comfortably as they walked toward the bonfire below. Jack guided her through the trees and toward the river, which roared in the background.

She scanned the area. "I never came here before," she said.

As they got closer, she heard her name. Calls from around the fireside welcomed her. She squinted to see who was there and looked up at Jack and smiled. "So this is the Tiger's Den," she said.

Terry Whitaker strode toward her and threw his arms around her. "I'm so glad to see you, Jessie. You're looking good. I saw Coach the other day and he asked about you."

"Thanks," she said, remembering that Terry had made the UGA football team. "How's school…and the Bulldogs?"

"The Bulldogs are great! We're playing in a bowl game this year. Hope to see you back in Athens soon."

Jessie leaned into Jack and placed her arm through his. "Jack has been telling me about school. I know I've missed a lot."

Terry caught Jack's eye. He knew how much his friend had been interested in Jessie from their early high school days. "Well, you know Jack's the man! I'm counting on you both coming to the Spring G-Day game."

The sound of footsteps coming down the abandoned driveway could be heard. Jessie turned to see Tom and Claire and Tom's voice rang out. "Jessie girl!" The three shared a group hug.

Claire embraced her friend Jessie a little longer and then held her at arm's length, inspecting her. "You look good, Jess. You have to come over to the house before I go back to Durham." A friend since childhood, Claire lived two doors up the street from the Reynolds. She had not seen Jessie since Carter's funeral.

Tom patted Jack on the back. "Wow! Good to see everyone. With so many cars we had to park down the street a ways. Didn't want to tip anyone off."

The "Tiger's Den" had always been a special meeting place for the rare few from Northwest High who knew its location. There were strict parking instructions: *Don't draw the attention of anyone passing the abandoned driveway on the street above.* Tom scanned the area. "The place still looks the same." He walked over to a large rock at the corner of the remains of an old fireplace and lifted it to uncover a small church key opener and held it up to the group. "Yep! It's still here!" The group cheered and raised their cans and bottles.

He popped the cap on his beer and led Claire to a perch close to the fire. She shared a sip from the bottle and then took her place on his lap. No time to waste—they hadn't seen each other for a while. Tom was in school at Vanderbilt in Nashville—Duke and Claire were a long way away.

Jessie leaned over to Jack. "Can we talk?" she whispered.

He nodded and together they headed to a quieter spot on the other side of the fire circle away from the others. He helped her up on a large stone and settled in beside her. Jessie thought of a similar stone at the Witches' Cave. Carter had boosted her up to it when they'd sneaked away from the crowd after his high school graduation at Chastain Park.

Jack waited for her to speak and then finally spoke himself. "You okay?"

She nodded and looked at the river. "I got a letter today…from a soldier at Fort Benning. A Sergeant Randall. He was the platoon leader in Carter's unit." She rubbed her chilly hands together and Jack took them in his to warm them. Jessie glanced up at him—it was as if she was seeing him for the first time. The unexplained feeling from earlier in the day washed over her again.

"Go on," he coaxed.

"He had gotten the names of family and friends of the men in his unit who'd been killed. He wrote some really nice things about Carter."

"I'm sure that was good to hear," said Jack. He put an arm around her and she leaned against him. "You know," she said, "after I read the letter, I went for a walk and ended up in the park at the place…you know, the place where Carter told me he'd enlisted."

Jack nodded. He knew the exact spot because it was also where Carter had asked him to take care of Jessie.

"I had this feeling," she said. "A feeling of peace that I can't describe."

He glanced down at their hands, still entwined. "Maybe in time you'll know what it means. That feeling, I mean. That was a special place for you and Carter. I know you went there a lot."

"Yeah. We had some wonderful times there. It was where he told me a lot about himself and his family. Each time it brought us closer. I wish I knew how to describe what I'm feeling."

"You can always tell me anything, Jess."

Jessie searched her heart and gazed into the fire. They sat silently until she cleared her throat, "Do you think maybe it was the sergeant's letter that caused it? You know, that feeling of peace?"

Jack shrugged his shoulders. "It could be," he said. He glanced over at the friends nearby joking, enjoying their beverages and telling their college stories. "You know that Georgia Day weekend Terry mentioned will be here before you know it. How about coming up? I'm sure they would have you a place to stay at the sorority house."

Jessie thought for a moment. "It would be good to see everyone back in Athens…and I know I need to let admissions know when I plan to return to classes." The fireside couples continued telling college stories and a feeling long since experienced bubbled up in Jessie. It felt good to laugh again.

Jack waited to see if Jessie would say more about the letter but her mood had obviously changed. And that was okay with him. Her head on his shoulder watching the river, the stars, the fire…was more than enough.

Chapter 6

Concerns about too much New Year's celebration in Cross Hill were never a worry for Sheriff Yates Bryan. He would monitor the evening activities by making several rounds up and down the corridors of Main Street in his cruiser. Each storefront and every other known public gathering spot would be checked. Nothing would get by him on his watch—he made it his business to know everyone in town and anyone else who frequented the surrounding area.

On one of his turns, he saw Roy Jasper making his way up the street in his Ford pickup. Yates rolled down his window. "Hey, Mr. Roy. Got your fireworks all ready for the farm this evening?"

Roy nodded. "Randalls are in town and hoping I could still find some ice for the family celebration," he replied. "Sargent Matt is stateside. He's here with Miss Christine and Miss Starr."

*Hmmm…*thought the sheriff. *Once again, Christine is here and nobody told me.*

Yates Bryan and Christine Chapman had been friends during her high school years when she'd spent summers on the family farm. Their relationship had grown to be more than friends the summer after her senior year but their romance had been interrupted when she'd suddenly returned to Wilmington without a word. The news of her marriage later to Mitch Randall had come as a disappointment to him. In his mind, there would never be another girl for him.

"Well, you tell them Happy New Year for me," said the sheriff.

"Will do. Happy New Year to you too. Fishing is pretty good down at the pond. Come on by anytime."

Roy pulled up to The General and was relieved the store was still open. He grabbed a basket and added several items to it along with the ice. On his way out, he waved to the clerk. "This is for the farm," he said, and the clerk nodded.

"I'll put it on the Chapman account."

The Chapman and Jasper family history dated to the early days of sharecropping. The Chapmans had been dedicated to helping the Jaspers have a better life. As an adult, Roy had become the caretaker for the homeplace and rewarded with a cabin near the roadway leading onto the farm. He made sure the property was maintained and the farmhouse clean and ready for family visits. He'd established a tradition of placing fishing poles on the front porch was a signal that the house was ready and waiting for weary travelers.

As a teen and in later years, Roy was often seen with a bottle in his overall pocket from which he slipped a quick sip when he thought no one was looking. Its label read "Southern Comfort." Then, when Christine and other young children came along, they shadowed Roy as he made his rounds, asking questions about the farm, his garden—and the bottle. Young Christine had asked, "Mr. Roy, why do you like your drink so much?"

"Oh, Miss Christine," he'd said, quickly returning the bottle to his overalls, "that's just my favorite sweet tea." She'd later given him the nickname "Comfort." The adults in town had soon adopted the name too.

The children would skip behind Comfort as he completed his chores in the barn and follow him out to the pasture, never letting him out of their sight. When they got older, visits to the farm included activities and trips down at the lake, and Comfort's "sweet tea" ceased to be seen and his demeanor changed, but the name had stuck.

At a Thanksgiving gathering years later, the Chapman family had surprised their cherished friend with a carved wooden plaque with "Comfort" on it and installed it on the mailbox. Thereafter, the farm would be known by his nickname as well.

Comfort felt gratitude for the Chapmans as he drove his truck up the gravel driveway toward the house. So much in his life had changed over the years. In celebration of Matt's homecoming and the family who had always been there for him, he would build a big fire and share a New Year's meal with the family at the pine dining table he had created in his workshop.

CHRISTINE RANDALL STOOD STIRRING A PAN of cooked apples and called to her son. "Matt? How's the ham looking?" she said. "Comfort will be back from the store soon and the vegetables are just about done."

Matt opened the oven and breathed in the aroma. "Hmmm, perfect!" he said, and smiled to himself. Every time he had opened his rations in the jungle or eaten at the mess hall at Fort Benning, he had dreamed of returning to his mother's home cooking. Nothing could match his mother's recipes, her touch, and her expressions of love. Love was something he had rarely known from anyone other than his mother and sister. Certainly not from his dad.

Christine called to her daughter too. "Starr, is the table set? Use Mama's china. She always liked us to put it out on special occasions. And…" she said, looking at her son, "this is definitely a special occasion. Our Matt is back safe and sound!"

The young sergeant walked through the farmhouse. It was just as he had remembered on his last stay before deployment. A Christmas wreath remained over the fireplace awaiting the family's delayed celebration. He stood and gazed at the shadow boxes filled with military medals—his grandfather's, father's, and now his.

He felt his mother's arm slip around his waist. "We're so proud of you, son," she said.

"Thanks, Mom," he said. "But I can't help but think of all the men we lost."

Not seeing her son during his year-long tour in Vietnam had been difficult. She nodded. "I hope your time here will bring you some peace, Matt. What you've dealt with," she hesitated, "God only knows. I'm not asking you to talk about it anymore than you want to."

"You know I've never been much for talking about my feelings, but the chaplain gave me some of their families' addresses and I've written some letters. He said writing my thoughts and condolences could be helpful."

Starr came into the room, carrying crystal goblets for their New Year's champagne toast. "Do you think you'll hear back from any of them?"

"Probably not. Lt. Thacker told me to be prepared though. He said losing my men was painful, but seeing the heartbreak of their families. would be too. But if it will help them, I want to do it. Maybe it will bring them closer to a sense of peace."

Starr was proud of her older brother, who had followed both their father and grandfather into military service. They'd always been close because of the regular moves from base to base during their childhoods. With little time to develop other close friends, they'd been each other's playmates. Now having been apart for a while—between his deployments and her trying to get a singing career off the ground—it had been more difficult to stay in touch.

When she finished setting the table, Starr took her guitar from its case and sat down to tune it. After dinner, she would sing some of her latest compositions for them. Starr's music had long been her passion, but she'd had diminishing success of late. Matt smiled at the sight. "Sis? Where to next? You haven't told me anything about your bookings." He stole a glance at their mother. "Staying out of trouble, aren't you?"

Christine made a face. From the time her children were small, she'd never known when the things Matt said about his sister were true or just a tease.

Comfort had stepped in from the doorway and placed his shopping bag on the kitchen counter. "Now Mr. Matt," he said. "You know Miss Starr can do no wrong!"

Starr strummed the guitar strings and reached for one key. "I am up and down the coast right now. Feeling sort of like a gypsy looking for a home. I may look for a new agent. The one in Charlotte hasn't given me much support over the last year."

Christine set the salt and pepper shakers on the table and nodded to Matt. "I told her that life is about change—that maybe she should be looking at doing something different."

Starr rolled her eyes. "I know, Mom. That's why I am planning a visit to Atlanta. I have an appointment with an agent there. Perry Michaels is his name. I got his card awhile back from a band that was playing at one of my gigs."

"Atlanta!" said Matt. "That's not far from Columbus. We should meet up while you're there." He paused. "Does this Perry know that your stage name is Starr *Chapman*?"

"He will. A lot of musicians use different names," she said, setting the guitar aside. "I'd rather talk about you. Here you are, the best-looking soldier there ever was with that physique. And you have your pilot's license, for pete's sake! When are you gonna find that someone who makes you question re-upping for another tour?"

"How did this get turned around to be about me?" He took the basket of rolls from his mother and added them to the table.

"Let's face it, you got all the good looks of the family and all the heart too. Mama and I—Comfort too—just want to see you happy. Isn't that right, Comfort?"

"You're gonna bring Comfort into this? How come you're not checking on *his* love life?" Matt laughed and made his way over to their caretaker to give his arm a shove.

Comfort shook his head and smiled. "Got me all I need right here. This farm and this family."

Christine smiled and emptied the bag of items from The General. "Dinner is almost ready. Comfort, I hope you saved a big place in that stomach of yours for dessert." She raised a cake stand with her one of her famous chocolate pound cakes.

Comfort pointed to his neck. "Oh, yes, ma'am—and a special spot for dessert up here!" Everyone laughed. They could count on him to remind them of all the good times spent on the farm with one of his special sayings. Christine moved to the kitchen to find the dessert plates. "Oh, and Miss Christine," he said. "Sheriff Bryan said to tell you Happy New Year." Christine hesitated at the kitchen window but said nothing.

A family tradition for the Chapmans was dinner by candlelight.

Comfort reached for matches to light the candles on the table and turned to Matt. "You think you'll have time for one of your flyovers of the farm?"

A soft expression crossed Matt's face. "Maybe I'll get you up there with me sometime, Comfort. It *is* a special sight from above to see this place."

"Oh, no," said Comfort. "Not me. Feet on the ground—that's me. I've had my share of saving grace. Not going to tempt the good Lord another time."

He blew out the match and they all stood in silence, looking at the table and thinking their own grateful thoughts. The home place, with its handmade quilts, canned fruits, vegetables and flowers from Comfort's garden, had always been a symbol of simple times and the lessons of love and forgiveness held deep in their hearts.

"Oh, Comfort! I almost forgot," said Christine. "We have a special guest coming in March. We want to be sure everything is prepared. He'll stay for several months probably."

Midnight approached and the family meal was complete. Christine brought four goblets to the table—three with champagne and one with water. Comfort took his water glass to join the family at the fireplace for a holiday toast. Matt looked at the framed medals on the mantel and back to his family and lifted his glass. "Here's to another year filled with the love of family and our hopes for lives of peace and happiness."

Chapter 7

Madeline opened the door for Jack and gave him her special hug. "Happy New Year…almost! You look especially handsome tonight, Jack."

He straightened his tie and smiled in acknowledgment of her welcome. Madeline called up the stairs to Jessie's bedroom to tell her that Jack had arrived and gestured toward the living room. "Have a seat, Jack. She'll be down in a minute. The New Year's Eve party at the Cherokee Club sounds wonderful."

Jack straightened his tie again. "Tom's parents arranged the invitation. I have to admit the original gathering at the Cabana Hotel was an option, but Tom insisted this would be more special. The club requires coat and tie. Everyone thought it would be nice to dress up for a change."

Jessie had reread Sgt. Randall's letter that afternoon and penned a reply. She was still trying to make sense of her thoughts and feelings and was excited about her date with Jack, but questions about her relationship with him kept coming to her. She licked the envelope and sealed it, and placed it on her bedside table for the next mail.

One last look in the mirror and application of lipstick, a few items for her small purse and she would be ready. She slipped the *One Day at a Time* medallion from Carter into one of the zippered pockets and headed downstairs.

Jessie entered the room and she turned to show her dress. "What do you think?"

Jack jumped to his feet. "Terrific!" he said.

Madeline grabbed Jessie's dress coat, which was draped over the arm chair nearby. "It's another cold night out."

"Yes, ma'am," said Jack. "Tom said the club added heaters on the terrace for tonight." He reached for the coat and held it open for Jessie.

Ladd joined them from the kitchen. "Be careful out there tonight and take care of our girl."

"Yes, sir. You can count on it."

Jack and Jessie made their way to his Volkswagen waiting in the driveway. "This brings back memories of prom," said Jessie.

Jack opened her door and smiled. "It does," he said.

She took her seat and looked up at him. "It's different, though," she said. "This time it's a real date."

Jack was caught by surprise. "It is," he answered. "Our first." He made his way to his side of car and imagined the night ahead. Jessie waited for him to close his door and turn on the ignition.

"But not our last?"

"No, not our last." He shifted gears to back out of the driveway and slowly head up the street. He rolled to a stop before reaching Northside Drive to make a turn toward their destination. He pointed between the two of them. "Jessica Reynolds, are you ready for this?"

A sensation of peace washed over her again. Jessie nodded yes and tears welled in her eyes.

"What is it?"

Jessie reached for his hand. "Thank you."

"For what?"

"For being you. For being here for me after all we've been through together."

Jack wiped a tear from her cheek. "Thank you for letting me be at the front of the line. "

Tom Caldwell's parents joined him and Claire at the entrance to greet their guests. The Cherokee Club sparkled with its festive decorations. Fresh flower arrangements adorned every table with 1967 party favors at each place. The girls found headbands created with stars and tinsel to wear. Missy Davis and Mike Martin sat at a table of high school friends and saw Jessie and Jack checking their coats. Missy nodded in their direction. "Mike, look. I always knew they would someday get together."

"Yep," said Mike. "Terry and I had a bet our senior year over whether Jack would ever get Jessie's attention."

Jessie turned to Jack. "Can you put my purse in your pocket?" He warmed at this simple sign of her comfort in their relationship and then felt a tap on his shoulder.

"Hi, Jack!" Their longtime high school friend, Sandy, was standing behind them.

"Sandy!" exclaimed Jessie.

"Oh, hey, Jessie," said Sandy barely diverting her eyes from Jack.

Happy to see her longtime friend, Jessie overlooked Sandy's cool reception. "It's good to see you," she said. "How's life in Knoxville?"

"Great...just great." Sandy's eyes remained focused on Jack.

Tom waved to Jessie and Jack and pointed to places reserved for them at the table in the center of the room. Jessie took Jack's hand and turned to Sandy. "We've got to get together while you're home, okay?"

"Yeah," said Jack. "Maybe we can all go to the Zesto? Like old times?" He escorted Jessie toward their table, ignoring Sandy's eyes, which were burning into their backs. The girl finally turned to join friends at a table across the room but glanced back to observe the couple again.

The band's lead singer announced a night of songs that had been popular over the past year. "This is a great song by the Four Tops called *Reach Out, I'll Be There.*"

Jack stood and stretched his hand out to Jessie. "Can I have this dance?" Jessie smiled and accompanied him to the dance floor, along with other couples at their table.

The evening was filled with laughter and festivities. "Our medley continues," said the lead singer. "Clap your hands with us." And the band sang "*Can't Help Myself.*" Jessie and Jack joined the couples at the stage and swayed to "*Baby, I Need Your Loving.*" Jessie was acutely aware of Jack's arms around her waist and the warmth of his touch.

The clock inched closer to midnight. During a slow dance, Jack whispered in Jessie's ear. "How's our first date?"

"A wonderful beginning," she said. Jack pulled her closer then leaned her back in a slow dip.

The microphone crackled. "Grab your date and your glass, my friends! It is time for our countdown!"

The couples returned to the table and Jack was suddenly nervous. He and Jessie had never kissed before.

"Ten, nine, eight…" Shouts could be heard around the room. Jessie turned to Jack in silence. He looked into her eyes and softly repeated the numbers.

"Happy New Year!" erupted from the friends at their table. While others kissed and celebrated, Jack stood looking at Jessie. She waited for what would come next. He stepped closer to her, but just as his lips almost touched hers, they heard Tom's voice ring out.

"Hey, everyone! Come join us! I'm glad you are with us tonight," he said. "I have an important question to ask." They turned back toward Tom and Claire and watched as he knelt in front of her. "You are my soulmate, my best friend," said Tom to Claire. "Being apart this year at school has shown me even more how much you mean to me." Everyone around the table gasped—they knew the direction Tom was heading. He pulled a ring box from his pocket and opened it. "Claire, will you marry me?"

Tears sprang to Claire's eyes and she nodded her head. "Yes, yes!"

Jack, Jessie and the others clapped and cheered as Tom placed an engagement ring on her finger and drew her in for an endless kiss.

Jack glanced at Tom's parents, who were smiling and clapping from afar. "Oh, now I understand why Tom was so insistent on the party being here at the club," he said.

Jessie leaned back against him with tears streaming down her face—both in happiness and disappointment. A year ago, all their friends were placing their bets that Jessie and Carter would be the first couple from their senior class to become engaged.

The band continued to play *Auld Lang Syne* as congratulations were expressed around the table. Claire glowed and showed the ring to the girls circling her.

Jack reached for Jessie's hand. "One more dance?" She followed him to the dance floor and, as he put his arms around her, he leaned down with his lips near her ear. "You okay?"

She tightened her arms around his shoulders and whispered back. "I'm happy for Tom and Claire."

Jack retrieved Jessie's coat and handed his ticket to the valet. He reached into his pocket and gave Jessie her purse. "I really am happy for them," she said.

When the valet returned in the Volkswagen, they climbed in and Jack pulled away from the valet stand. He drove down to the vacant parking area overlooking the club's golf course. They sat as the heater warmed up and Jack searched for the right words to break the silence. Finally, he took a deep breath. "First dates can be a little awkward," he said.

Jessie tried to laugh. "Yeah, but usually there's not a proposal."

She rubbed her hands together for warmth. Jack reached over and put his hands around hers. "Better?" he asked.

"Much better," she responded.

It was Jessie's turn for a deep breath. "Jack, I hope you can be patient with me."

"Take all the time you need, Jess. I'm here." He put the car in gear and they rode silently down Paces Ferry toward Jessie's home, down Longwood Drive, and into her driveway.

"I go back to Athens soon," he said. She nodded and made a sad face. He planted a gentle kiss on her cheek. "Happy New Year, Jess." He gestured between the two of them again like he had at the beginning of their night together. "Are you *still* ready for this?"

"You've always been here for me, Jack. I don't know what I would have done without you." He questioned her with his eyes and could only wonder if she meant as a friend...or more.

Jessie gave him the answer with a soft and lingering kiss to his lips. "Happy New Year, Jack."

Chapter 8

The morning was brisk with clear skies, and Ladd Reynolds stepped out onto the front porch to see if the morning newspaper was anywhere in sight on the front sidewalk. *The New Year's Day edition must be running late*, he thought. He turned to go back in the house for a hot cup of coffee.

"Mr. Reynolds!" came a shout. He looked up the street to see a hand waving back and forth. Claire was bouncing across the yards between them heading in his direction, her breath visible in the cold morning air. "Mr. Reynolds! Is Jessie awake? Did she tell you my news?"

Ladd lifted a hand and waved back. "No, she came in late last night. I heard her stirring a little earlier, though," he said.

With pride, she extended her left hand to show the emerald cut diamond ring with side baguettes. "Tom gave it to me last night at the club! It was his grandmother's. Isn't it beautiful?"

Ladd looked down at her hand. The morning sun glistened off the white gold and stone family heirloom. "It sure is. Congratulations, Claire! You and Tom are a special pair and such good friends to Jessie."

"With all the excitement last night I didn't get time to talk to her."

Ladd smiled and opened the front door. "Come in. She's upstairs. You know the way."

Jessie stood at her bathroom sink brushing her hair when she heard someone running up the stairs. She stepped out in time to see her bedroom door burst open and Claire beaming.

"I couldn't wait to see you this morning!"

Jessie gave a big hug to her best friend ever.

"Tom and I didn't get much of a chance to see you last night after his BIG surprise."

Jessie grinned. "You were surrounded by everyone. I knew we would get our time together soon." She laughed. "I just didn't know it would be before breakfast!"

They both settled on Jessie's twin bed and Claire extended her hand to show her friend the ring more closely. "Tom never mentioned his grandmother's ring. I won't ever take it off!" She looked down to admire it once again.

Jessie thought of the time she and Carter had been apart when he'd been at Bradford College. "I know it has been hard for you both being at different schools."

"Yeah. Duke and Vanderbilt. What were we *thinking*?" She waved her hand. "Anyway, *this* changes that!"

"I'm so happy for you…and Tom," said Jessie. "You both have been so supportive to me."

"And you to us. That is one reason I'm here. I want you to be one of my bridesmaids!"

Jessie smiled. "Of course!"

"And…" continued Claire, "I am going to need your help. We want to have the wedding at the end of May!"

Jessie was stunned. "May?!"

Growing up, the girls had played dress-up as brides with their make-believe grooms. They had overheard Jessie's older siblings talk about all the details and arrangements required for an Atlanta society wedding.

Jessie shook her head. "Is it possible? I can only imagine with Tom's family connections the kind of wedding that you will have! Is there enough time?"

Claire shrugged. "I couldn't sleep last night thinking of all the details. As it was, my mother was waiting up for Tom and me to come home last night. Tom was so sweet to have asked for her blessing and one from my dad earlier…you know, with the divorce and all. We couldn't do this—a wedding, finishing school, and all—without all our parents' support. That was part of the conversation with them. Completing college was part of the deal."

"Doesn't Tom want to go to med school too?"

"That's the plan. I know it won't be easy, but we can do anything as long as we're together."

Jessie felt a twinge in her heart and couldn't disguise it.

"Oh, Jessie," said Claire. "I hope you know how much my heart hurts if this causes you more sadness about Carter."

"Don't worry about that. This is *your* moment. It's a happy time for you and Tom and I'm here to celebrate with you in every way."

Jessie was thrilled to hear Crow's voice on the phone. "Happy New Year, Jess," he said.

"Crow, how are you? It's been too long," said Jessie.

"Doing fine. Brandi says to tell you hello."

"I would love to see you both. How's the band?"

"I talk to them now and again, but we're not playing together anymore. We all decided to move on from The Playboys. It was good while it lasted. Things were just not the same, you know?" He paused.

"You can say it, Crow. You mean not the same without Carter, don't you?"

"Yeah." He paused again. "How are you? Is this a good time to talk?"

"Sure. What's going on?"

"Well, I had a call from our agent, Perry Michaels. We stay in touch. You know, in case something comes up that had the band's name on it. He would like to meet with you. It...it has to do with Carter."

It was Jessie's turn to pause. "Perry Michaels wants to talk to me?"

"Yeah. I was wondering if we could find a time we could go to Perry's office and meet with him."

"What's this about?"

"Perry can explain that better than me."

Jessie rose early to take some treats to the children's ward at Egleston. It did her good to go—the children looked forward to her visits and always requested music first thing. Their joy and laughter were gentle reminders of the words of Carter's last letter...t*o bring hope to the other lives she would touch.*

Madeline heard a car in the driveway and peeked out the front door to see Jack coming up the walk. She stepped back and opened it wide. "I'm sorry, Jack. Jessie went out to Egleston to take some treats to the children."

Disappointment washed across his face. "Could you give this to her from me? Tell her I had to head back to school early." He handed a package to her.

"Oh, Jack... I know she will be sorry she missed you."

WHEN JESSIE RETURNED TO THE HOUSE, her mother called to her from the living room. "I can't believe you just missed Jack!" She pointed to the coffee table and a gift wrapped in silver foil with a purple ribbon. "He left this for you."

Jessie sat on the sofa and looked at the box with wonder and sadness. Jack had left it without saying goodbye.

"What is it?" asked her mother.

Jessie read the note attached. *I hope these will keep you warm until we see each other again. Love, Jack.*

She unwrapped the gift box to find a pair of knitted white gloves. Her initials were embroidered at the wrist.

Chapter 9

The fellowship hall of the Sandy Springs Methodist Church buzzed. A special meeting of the leadership had been called and the bishop was coming to speak. The new year had begun for the flourishing congregation and those arriving assumed it was a planning discussion about upcoming ministry changes—due to the ever-increasing congregation size, extra services were now scheduled to accommodate seating. Representatives of the staff parish committee and church council were there along with others in positions of authority. Bobby Powell, who had been asked to lead a committee, was seated near the front.

When Bishop Clemons arrived, he was alone. Those in the room looked around—it was highly unusual for the bishop to be there without their pastor, Rev. Stephen Hamilton. The bishop took the floor and called the meeting to order.

"My friends, thank you for coming. I'm grateful for your presence tonight." He glanced around the room. "I don't think we need to go through any formal agenda other than to say that I am here to bring forth a recommendation concerning Rev. Hamilton." A rumble passed through the crowd. "We have been more than impressed with Stephen's ministry here and it is our belief, as I am sure you would agree, that he is ready to take on a higher role in our conference."

Bobby was stunned. The thought of losing his most trusted counselor and family adviser was almost too much to fathom. Memories washed over him—all the times spent with him over the years since losing his Grandfather Crawford and then Carter in Vietnam. He'd officiated at his and Marie's recent wedding. Both he and Marie would be heartbroken to learn that Stephen might not be the person who would one day dedicate their children to the church.

"This church has grown under Rev. Hamilton's nurture," continued the bishop. "You should all be proud of the impact you've made in this community. We will work with you to find a new pastor soon." He paused. "In the meantime, however, the conference has recommended a sabbatical for him first so he'll have some time to get away and rest."

The room was silent. What had started as a time of fellowship turned solemn. Bishop Clemons asked if there were questions and seeing no one raise a hand, he assured the crowd he would be available to meet with them later and closed the meeting.

The church members slowly made their exit. Bobby headed home to share the news with Marie. On the way, his thoughts turned to Jessie—he would need to tell her the news too.

"Bobby! Come in!" exclaimed Madeline. She opened her arms and gave him a hug. "It's so good to see you. How's Marie? We haven't seen you since the wedding. It has been too long."

Bobby smiled, but he couldn't hide the fact he was there to deliver somber news. "Marie is great," he said. "She's working hard around the house, giving it her special touches." He described a couple of things Marie had accomplished and then took a deep breath.

"I know she will be hearing from Rev. Hamilton, but I felt it important to tell Jessie the news first." Concern rose on Madeline's face, and he hurried to explain. "Everything's okay, Mrs. Reynolds. It's just that the reverend is leaving the church. Word like that travels fast, you know."

"Oh," she said. She knew how much Stephen Hamilton meant to Bobby and Marie…and especially to her daughter. Jessie had spent numerous hours in grief counseling with him after Carter's funeral. "When did this happen?"

"The bishop told us last night. The conference is placing him on sabbatical first so he'll have some time to get away and rest."

Jessie appeared in the doorway of the living room. "Get away? Who is going away?"

Bobby turned to her. "Rev. Hamilton. He's leaving the church. The conference is recognizing him with a new position."

Madeline pointed to the living room chair across the room—the same seat where Coach O'Connor had sat when he'd brought Carter's last letter to Jessie. "Have a seat, Bobby."

The three sat for a moment unable to voice their sadness. "I don't know what to say," said Jessie. "But I guess this must be a good thing for him."

Madeline nodded. "We all have depended on him for so much, and I know there are many others who have done the same."

"There will never be anyone else who has meant as much to our family," said Bobby.

"We must have him over for dinner before he leaves," said Madeline. "You and Marie and, of course, Coach O'Connor."

Jessie nodded in agreement. Bobby stood up and gave her a goodbye embrace.

"Thank you for coming to tell me, Bobby."

When Ladd got home later that evening, Madeline gave him the news. "I'm worried about how Rev. Hamilton's leaving will affect Jessie's recovery. He's been a lifeline to her."

Ladd put his arms around his wife. "Yes, and to so many others."

THE CHEROKEE CLUB HAD OPENED FOR the day. Coach Paul O'Connor and Dr. Frank Caldwell sat waiting. When Stephen arrived for their regular Friday morning round of golf, they greeted each other. "You guys ready for some some serious competition?" asked Frank.

Stephen pointed to the bench area outside. "I know we usually check our calendars when we finish, but I need to tell you guys about a development."

"Sure thing," said Frank. "What's up?"

"This was just announced at our church council meeting Wednesday night, and I wanted to tell you as soon as possible before the word got out any further—the rumor mill is buzzing."

"What's up?" asked Paul.

"Might as well not beat around the bush," said Stephen. "I'm being reassigned by the conference."

Both of his friends looked at him in shock. "I…uh…don't know what to say," said Frank.

"I don't either, really. It's happening pretty quickly," said Stephen. "What I didn't expect was that I would begin with a sabbatical."

Paul thought of all the times Stephen had come to his rescue in times of need and sadness. He remembered the time of their first meeting, sitting together in the Piedmont Hospital chapel when he'd learned his wife's diagnosis was terminal. He thought of all the nights on the sidelines and in the locker rooms at the high school football games after Stephen became the team's chaplain and all their conversations about Carter Powell and the minister's words at Carter's funeral.

"I know I've depended on you, Stephen, and I can't imagine what it's been like for you taking care of your whole congregation all these years."

Frank Caldwell nodded his head. "We've never had conversations this deep before, but I have to say that you more than deserve this time of sabbatical. I have wondered how you've done what you have at a 24/7 pace."

"Well," said Stephen, "we all hold the lives of others in our hands." "Paul, taking care of the young people you coach and teach can be daunting. And Frank, you face every day the responsibility of the health of so many." He paused. "I never really gave it a thought until recently, but the bishop is right. My well has been running dry. It's almost empty."

He glanced at the coach and doctor. "Take care of your own wells, my friends. The bishop helped me unpack it all when we met last week. He asked me some simple questions. 'How do you have fun?' and 'How do I take care of myself?' Initially, I felt like I was being punished by the decision. You know, being sent away from the ones I love. Especially you guys." He swallowed hard. "But he assures me it will bring a renewed perspective for me. That a sabbatical will help to refill *my* well."

Frank nodded. "And I have to add, except for our golf outings, I've never seen you take time for yourself. What I mean is that you've never taken time for any kind of relationship outside the church! You too, Paul. I know that you still miss Ann a lot. It's time you both looked to the future and found someone to share it with you. Don't dare tell her I said this," he said, grinning, "but I wouldn't be able to do what I do without Tricia."

"Okay, now. How did I get brought into this?" said Paul.

The three friends laughed and then Frank shook his head. "Seriously, you both need to focus more on your personal lives. Tricia has said it to me more times than I can count. Y'all have no idea how many times I've stopped her from trying to fix you both up with somebody."

They both smiled at Frank, but the mood was somber. The bishop had raised the same question with Stephen, knowing the glass house ministers often live in and the typical rumor mill that is a part of a minister's life. Paul had had the same conversation many times with his long-time faculty friend, Laura Laney. After Ann's death, she and her husband, Carl, had been on his case.

The marshal called their tee time, giving both Stephen and Paul a reprieve—for the moment. They each grabbed their clubs and headed for the first tee. But the seeds had been planted. Each in their own minds considered that their lives were about to change.

Chapter 10

"Randall!" Matt heard the call from the other end of the barracks and stepped from his partitioned cubicle. His assignment at Fort Benning had been extended and he'd been working with Lt. Thacker on plans for a future assignment.

The sergeant walked toward a private distributing mail. The private handed him an envelope and continued his rounds.

Matt scanned the envelope. The return address wasn't familiar but the handwriting, calligraphic grabbed his attention. He slipped a finger underneath the flap and opened the letter.

> *Dear Sgt. Randall,*
>
> *First of all, thank you for your thoughtfulness to write about Carter. I apologize for the time it has taken me to respond. I have struggled with accepting his loss and through the love of my family and friends I am dealing with the denial that continues to haunt me. I have a deep faith and trust that time will heal the wounds*

my heart still feels every time I see or touch a remembrance of him.

I will treasure the words of your letter which brings hope for my tomorrows knowing that I once had the love of a special man. We knew him in different ways, but I know we both share in his commitment to God, family, and country.

Peace and safety be with you in service and protection for those values we hold so dear.

Sincerely,

Jessica Reynolds

Matt folded the letter and put it into his pocket. He walked down the hallway to the command offices. Lt. Thacker's door was always open to his men. No one appreciated it more than Matt did.

When he reached the lieutenant's doorway, he stopped and saluted. "Sir, is there still a detail in Atlanta on the schedule sheet?"

The lieutenant picked up a folder and scanned its contents. "No detail listed, but one of the recruitment centers on Ponce de Leon has asked for additional help. You interested?"

Matt thought for a moment of about his sister's plan to visit a new booking rep in Atlanta. A temporary post, even at a recruitment center, might be good therapy for him, and he'd be able to spend some time with Starr. "Maybe..." he said. He touched the letter in his pocket and nodded his head. "Actually, sir, yes, I am."

Chapter 11

S tephen Hamilton stood packing the last of his books and belongings at the church office. He picked up the wedding picture of Bobby and Marie Powell with him in front of the Crawford memorial stained-glass window, carefully wrapped it in tissue, and placed it on top of the last box.

He wandered into the sanctuary and looked around the room where he'd spent so much time during the past few years. He had taken advantage of many opportunities to say goodbye to members of his congregation, but none threatened to be as emotional as the final dinner that evening at Ladd and Madeline Reynolds' home. Walking through their front door brought back all the times of joy and sorrow he had shared within those walls. Theirs had become the vision of "home" he hoped to have for himself someday. When Madeline had extended the invitation, he had asked her to make it an intimate gathering of nine—the people involved in some of his most poignant memories would be there.

He returned to his office, picked up the box, and taking one last look around, closed the door.

LADD WELCOMED STEPHEN INSIDE AS THE rest of the minister's friends stood to greet him. Trish Caldwell and Marie Powell surrounded him with hugs. Frank and Bobby shook his hand. Paul O'Connor smiled over their shoulders with a "thumbs up"—a sign of support for his best friend's new journey ahead. Madeline and Jessie were in the kitchen putting the finishing touches on the roast beef supper. Preparing the dinner had been an act of holiness in Madeline's eyes—she'd taken great efforts to create Stephen's favorite meal.

Once the food had been placed on the table, Ladd seated everyone and called for a moment to share a word and blessing.

"This is a momentous occasion, although bittersweet for us. We celebrate our friend Stephen and a much-deserved recognition of his ministry. He has made a lifelong impact and has been a gift to each of the lives gathered around this table. I hope in some ways we have been the same for him. Stephen, know this is not a goodbye, but a celebration— know that our paths will continue to cross and that our prayers go with you." Ladd raised his glass amid murmurs of "Amen" from the others.

Stephen raised his glass as well. "You are family for me. I will never be far away." He looked at each person around the table, his eyes settling on Jessie and the tears streaming down her face. "I know in my heart this will always be home. Thank you for who you are and what you mean to me."

After dessert, Madeline appeared with a wrapped package. "Stephen, we know you have much to do before you leave in the morning. This is something we all wanted you to have as a remembrance of our friendship. With each use, we trust it will be a sacred token of those who love you as you share it with others you bless in the days ahead."

Stephen unwrapped the package and was overwhelmed with the thoughtfulness of his friends. He gently removed several layers of tissue to find a beautiful clay communion set. The glazed plate, cup and pitcher was a one-of-a-kind creation by a local potter and would be a cherished reminder of his Atlanta friends and his journey with them.

Principal Lewis Kelley heard a knock and looked up to see Coach O'Connor standing in his doorway. It was late afternoon and most students were gone for the day.

"Mind if I come in?" said the coach.

Kelley saw the seriousness on his colleague's face. "Sure, Paul. How's it going?"

The coach closed the door and sat down. "I gotta tell you where I am right now. I want to be honest as I know you want your faculty to be."

"Of course. I do and I've always trusted that—especially with you."

The coach sighed. "My good friend and our football team's chaplain, Stephen Hamilton, leaves this week. Knowing much about his work and life has given me a lot to think about in my own life. He helped me a lot when I lost Ann and…last year when we lost Carter Powell."

"He will be greatly missed around here."

"Yes, he will. In fact, that's what I want to talk to you about. Stephen was given a sabbatical as part of his leaving. The church recognized some burnout in him and a need for replenishment…and a change."

"Okay."

"I am thinking I need a change as well. Replenishment. More to my life. We haven't announced a summer schedule yet and I wanted you to know that I have decided I won't be having a sports camp here as usual. I need to take a sabbatical of my own."

Chapter 12

Stephen Hamilton had packed his car early to allow for a cool start for the drive to Cross Hill and the farm where he would spend his sabbatical. He realized now that the years and the congregation he so loved had sapped his energy as had been true for many clergy members. Bishop Clemons had recognized the symptoms in his annual visit with him. The growing suburban Atlanta church would need to bless this time of replenishment along with the recognition of his time to move to a new assignment.

The morning air lifted his spirits. The roads from Atlanta to Laurens County were worn in some places, but the views of countryside farmland, lakes and forests filled him with renewed hope. He glanced down at the seat. Beside him lay stacks of books he had intended to read over the last several years, and a twinge of guilt surged through him. The bishop had challenged him to stretch himself during the three months and do things outside his normal pattern. Reading these books, all with a spiritual element, did not qualify.

"Don't think you have to prove something to others about your time away," the bishop had told him. "It's the mistake too many make in trying to justify their sabbaticals."

Stephen had nodded his head as they spoke in his office that day in settling on the terms. But he had yet to accept that he could stop his usual habits "cold turkey."

He passed a sign for "Adams Produce"—a local stand ahead selling vegetables, fruits and boiled peanuts. It was early in the season and the sign was weathered and old, but he thought it would be a good time to take a break from the miles of driving.

The stand soon appeared on the right side of the road with a truck parked next to it piled high with crates and baskets. Vegetables and various types of seasonal produce, jams and relishes were displayed on a wooden bench. A man stood behind the bench and stoked a fire under a large black kettle.

When Stephen pulled off the highway, he couldn't help but notice a small-framed church across the road with a carefully-manicured cemetery and churchyard. The grass was mowed to a respectful perfection.

An earthy voice caught his attention. "Can I help you? We have some nice boiled peanuts today." The man scooped up a ladle full of the nuts and pointed to the empty container sizes for sale. In his other hand was a paper plate of sliced apples. "Have a piece," he continued. "Sweet as can be."

Stephen tasted a sample and smiled. "That is about the best apple I have ever tasted."

The farmer straightened his stance with pride. "You're not from around these parts, are you?" Stephen was surprised at the man's question and the farmer grinned at his expression. "Nice shoes and clean tires. It's a dead giveaway."

Stephen chuckled. "No. I'm on my way up toward Laurens County." He paused and took another slice of apple. "You're a good salesman. I'll take some apples and some of your peanuts. Maybe some jam, too."

The farmer placed the items in a paper bag. "Here you go. I threw in some of my tomatoes. We can grow them in these parts almost year-round. I got me a nice greenhouse. They're great for slicing. The wife even gives me a slice with my breakfast!"

As he opened his trunk to make room for his purchases, Stephen looked again across the road at the small church and made peace with the fact he would be worshipping in a different way the next day. He got into his car and checked the South Carolina map before starting the engine. He raised his hand to the farmer, all the while thinking he should put the roadside conversation into his journal as potential future sermon material.

His drive continued until he saw another weathered sign with the words "Camp Greenwood" on it. A newer sign was attached at the bottom announcing dates and ages of campers for the upcoming summer months. When he passed Lake Greenwood, he recognized it as a landmark the bishop had mentioned. The farm he was headed for was a family retreat Bishop Clemons had visited several times for his own health and renewal.

The signal light flashed its caution as Stephen drove slowly through the heart of the town of Cross Hill. At the intersection was a gas station with a single pump and a grocery store called The General. In front of the store were four rocking chairs and a bench with wooden crates stacked to one side. Through the trees further down the road, he could see the cedar shingles of a church steeple. Children skipped down a dirt-worn path along the roadside. *They don't have to worry about traffic like in Atlanta,* he thought.

A little further on, he saw a sign promoting the Cross Hill Garden Shop in front of a white picket fence and another store called the Mercantile. He thought about the provisions he'd packed that morning—they would suffice for the next few days, but he was sure he'd visit there soon.

But for now, he simply hoped to locate the farmhouse road. He'd been told by the bishop to look for a green mailbox with the name "Comfort" on it. When he finally spied it, he turned and drove down a long gravel road.

On the left was a tree-lined pond. Horses grazing in a pasture surrounded by tended fences lifted their heads at the sound of his vehicle. Stephen stopped briefly and rolled down his car window to look at them. He picked up his handwritten instructions and reread them. He was to pass a tin-roofed cabin across from the lake and continue straight to the end of this road.

When he rounded the last corner, he sighed. There among the pecan trees sat a farmhouse to behold—a spot that would be his home for the next several months. A string of crepe myrtles preparing for summer blooms stood off to one side. A gated garden was visible to the right of a circular driveway. Across the grounds, the late afternoon sun glistened through tree branches. A covey of doves sprang from tall grasses, and he stopped to watch their ascent.

A trimmed stone walkway led to a freshly painted porch, adorned by an American flag. Pine rockers sat waiting for someone to take a seat and a fishing pole leaned next to the door. Stephen touched the cane rod, appreciating its welcome.

Elizabeth Satterfield's Saturdays brought her a welcome rest from teaching. On the weekends, she switched gears to garden and attend to her family's business. She had never dreamed of living anywhere other than Cross Hill—upon graduating with a degree in elementary education from the College of Charleston, she'd returned to a third-grade teaching position at the Ford Elementary School in nearby Laurens. Charleston had its attractions and advantages, and dating came easily for her. But most boys she met in college had goals of a city life that didn't match her call to return to the Upstate.

She'd brought her passion for young children to her lesson plans and experiences growing up with her older brother Jeb—fishing, hunting, swimming, and horseback riding among them—that she used to captured her students' imaginations. She'd taken her class on field trips to state parks and nurseries and allowed them to try their hands at cooking foods grown in their gardens.

Elizabeth's parents had started the Mercantile and she had created the garden shop next door as part of a summer project during her senior year in high school. It had grown to become a favorite place for nature and gardening lovers and people drove from Greenville, Columbia, Charleston—even Charlotte—to see the store's latest display of plants, flowers and garden accessories.

Her brother Jeb had gone to Charleston for college too, attending The Citadel. Given his no-frills upbringing, he'd easily managed the tough military Corps of Cadets regime. Jeb's aspirations for a military career had been cut short by a horseback riding injury, but the moral code of the "long gray line" had served him well—he'd become a leader in the town.

Now, with both of their parents gone, Jeb had responsibility for the upkeep of the Satterfield farm. Their horses needed extra attention and he'd asked Comfort Jasper to stable their horses at the Randall place. And together, the Satterfield siblings managed the Mercantile and the Garden Shop.

Jeb watched a young woman shopping, carefully noting the price of each item she took from the shelf. The woman's son approached the counter—he had obviously saved his money for candy—and made a selection. "That's my favorite too," said Jeb to the boy as he opened the cash register. "I tell you what. Today is Favorite Candy Day. That means you get an extra treat with your purchase!" The boy's eyes grew big, and he reached over the counter to receive Jeb's offering.

The boy's mother overheard the exchange and stepped from behind the shelf. "We don't take handouts," she said.

"No handouts," called Jeb. "It's a new store promotion. You can ask my sister over there." He cut his eyes to Elizabeth, who was arranging flowers in the back.

"That's right," she said. "It's a new promotion for today only." The woman glanced in her direction and went back to her shopping. When she was done, Jeb rang up the purchases and watched as the mother and son left the store.

Elizabeth joined him at the front of the store. "Do you know them?"

"No," said Jeb. "He's just another one of the children I see frequently around town. They don't have much. Since the mill closed, more and more families are just scraping by. And the kids get the short end of it all."

"Yeah, you're right," she said. "At school, we've started talking about ways we can support these children. Summer is coming. We're all concerned once school is out they won't have enough to eat."

A bell on the store door signaled the entrance of another customer and the siblings looked up to see Sheriff Bryan.

"Hi, Liz," he said. "I'm here to help you carry the flowers to church."

"I'm almost finished."

"Sounded like you and Jeb were having a serious discussion when I came in."

"Sorta." Elizabeth walked to the window and pointed. "That woman and her son were just in. Jeb and I were talking about summer coming and the fact that a lot of my students may be hungry. They won't have a school lunch to depend on. They'll need something special to keep them occupied…and maybe feed them at the same time."

"I know what you mean," said Yates. He watched the mother and child walk down the street. "The more time some kids have on their hands, the more opportunities there are for trouble to find them."

STEPHEN BROUGHT IN A FEW THINGS and then explored the farmhouse. His books found homes here and there on end tables and on a bedroom dresser. He fought the urge to use the kitchen table as a desk—it would be so easy for him to return to his habit of using it as a place to work and write sermons. *No,* he thought, *this table will remain a place for mealtime only.* He did, however, place his new communion set in its center.

He stepped into the kitchen. A large box of golden beeswax taper candles sat next to a variety of candlesticks. A handful of wooden matches lay in a simple piece of pottery on the kitchen counter. On the stove was a black iron skillet and a hooked potholder hung from the handle of an adjacent drawer.

Two large stoneware mugs waited beside a jar of coffee beans and a manual grinder. He removed the lid on the jar, drew in a deep breath, and smiled, anticipating the next morning. He planned to sit in one of the front porch rockers and sip a fresh cup while enjoying his new view.

Down a hallway, he found two bedrooms, both with windows

overlooking a rose garden. A bath between the bedrooms was supplied with a stack of fluffy green towels balanced on a market bench next to a claw foot tub. Blocks of handmade soap filled a glass jar, all labeled with The Mercantile logo.

He mused as he wandered that preparation for his stay had been well thought out—simple but everything he needed. In his mind, he heard Bishop Clemons's words about embracing the simplicity of life. Maybe there was something to it.

On his return to the cozy living room with its stone fireplace, he felt weariness set in. The emotions of saying goodbyes, closing a chapter of his life, and a long drive had descended on him, and he laid his head on goose down pillows neatly arranged on the sofa and drifted to sleep. Hours later, he woke to a darkened room and an empty stomach calling to be fed.

Chapter 13

Before now, Jessie had not been to Perry Michaels's Ponce de Leon Avenue office. She was impressed with the images of famous clients on the wall of the reception area. An impeccably dressed receptionist greeted her and Crow and led them to a conference room. "Mr. Michael's is expecting you. He'll be right with you."

The agent appeared and extended his hand. "Good to see you, Crow! And this must be Miss Reynolds."

Jessie nodded. "Yes, I am," she said.

"I remember you now," he said. "You were there when the Playboys left for their tour." She nodded again and looked around the conference room. More pictures of famous clients arm-in-arm with Perry hung on the walls. She and Crow sat down beside each other across from a stack of folders.

Michaels sat down and pulled his chair up closer to the table. "I guess there's no reason for me to delay explaining the reason for our meeting. In particular with you, Miss Reynolds. I spoke with Crow before but he thought it best I explain."

Perry removed a sheet from a folder and placed it on the table in front of Jessie. She looked to Crow and back to the agent. The handwriting on the envelope took her breath away. "I received this letter from Carter Powell in late August," he said, "with a note attached." Jessie looked down. The word "Hope" was written at the top of the tablet.

"I don't understand."

"I thought you needed to see it for yourself. These are the lyrics to a song. I think they have potential and I'm working to find the right person to put it to music."

Jessie frowned and shook her head. "I still don't understand what I have to do with it, Mr. Michaels." She looked at Crow.

"You need to see the other part, Jess," he said. The agent nodded and handed her a handwritten note. She closed her eyes, reminded of all the notes Carter had written to her. She unfolded it and read.

> *"Mr. Michaels – I am leaving for military service soon. I have had these words in me for a long time. I would ask for your assistance to find a musician who could add music if you agree it has value. If you do and you can, I have only one request. In the event that something happens to me, all rights, royalties and privileges are to be assigned to Jessica Elaine Reynolds. The song is for her.*
>
> *Thank you, Carter Powell*

Jessie read the words of the song and looked at Crow. "He wrote that while we were on our summer tour," he said.

She turned back to the agent. "But what does this mean?"

"Who knows?" answered Perry. "Like I said, I want to find the right musician, and in the meantime, I thought you should be aware. If the song happens to become a hit, you would receive the royalties. I have copies of both documents. The originals are yours." He stood up and closed the folder. "Forgive me, but I have another appointment. Feel free to call me with any questions."

Jessie nodded, dazed. She stood to leave and Crow held her chair and then guided her through the door and into the reception area.

Perry nodded to a young woman waiting with a guitar case. "Come in, Miss Chapman," he said.

"You can call me Starr," the woman replied.

"Guess what, Matt! I have a new agent!" whispered Starr into the payphone in the lobby of Perry Michael's office.

"That's great, Sis!" said Matt. "By the way, I have a spare room with your name on it and I would love the company when you're in Atlanta." When Matt had arrived in Atlanta, he'd rented a furnished apartment. "This is a big city and I'm not acquainted with things here yet. We'll take advantage of your time here to see the sights."

Starr held the telephone closer to her mouth. "We're taking a break, so all the contract signing and stuff may take a while. Any female introductions yet?"

Matt chuckled. "I just arrived, Sis! No introductions. Besides, what good would it be? This assignment is only temporary and I could be deployed anytime. You know I can't let anything tie me down."

"You have a lot to offer, Matt. God only knows you got the best of the genes in the family."

"This will be good for you to take some time for yourself, too."

"We'll see. For now, it is all business and my career," she answered. "I'll see you later."

It had not taken Matt long to unpack and get acquainted with his surroundings. He took his lunch break to make a trip to the A&P nearby to stock the refrigerator and pantry to prepare for Starr's visit.

As he pushed his cart around the store, he watched shoppers check vegetables for freshness. Living on the base had meant he didn't have to think about grocery shopping, so it felt strange. This wasn't the only chasm that combat had created between him and the reality of a normal life. He needed to tread carefully to step back into a life free from the constant sense of danger he knew too well.

THE ARMY ENLISTMENT OFFICE WAS DOWN the street from Perry's office so that afternoon, the door of the office opened and Starr appeared holding a bottle of champagne. "We are going to celebrate tonight! Perry Michaels signed me for an ongoing gig HERE! I can't believe it."

Matt grinned. "That's great!"

"Perry even gave me some lyrics and asked me to work on the music for them. How cool is that?"

"Pretty cool," said Matt.

"So, I guess I *will* have to stay with you for a while if it's still okay?"

Matt grinned again. "Are you kidding me? I'm looking forward to the company. Besides, we still have a lot of catching up to do!" He looked at the champagne. "And a lot of celebrating! Let's call Mom and give her the good news."

"Oh, and get this! The lyrics of that song I mentioned? They were written by a soldier."

Chapter 14

Jessie had accepted Jack's invitation to come to Athens for the G-Day game and all the Panhellenic celebrations and Linda had called to confirm that her "little sister" could stay with her in the Alpha Chi house.

Lots of festivities were planned for the weekend, but most of all, Jessie couldn't wait to be with Jack. Pulling her suitcase out of the closet, she opened it on her bed. She reached for her pajamas along with her pledge tee shirt and a pair of shorts to wear.

Her mother appeared at her bedroom door. "Your dad has filled the gas tank for your trip."

"Are you sure you won't need your car?" Jessie asked her mother.

"I am sure. And it will be better than the train from the Emory station."

Jessie held up a dress. "I'm taking this for the game on Saturday."

Her mother glanced into the suitcase. "Is that a bathing suit you're packing?"

"Yes. It's hard to know what to take. We might sit out back of the sorority house to get some sun." She held up a pair of cut-off jeans. "I have a pair of these too just in case. Jack said we might spend an afternoon at Barnett Shoals with some of his fraternity brothers and their dates."

She opened her dresser for one final look and saw the box of her memories of Carter. She felt a whisper to her heart and turned back to her mother. "I think I have everything."

Ladd was waiting outside next to Madeline's Chevy when mother and daughter came out of the house. He took the suitcase, placed it in the trunk, and opened the driver's door for her.

Jessie climbed in and rolled down the window. "Thanks, Dad," she said.

Ladd was encouraged to see his daughter venturing out, taking a new step in her recovery. "Now, mind the speed limit and look both ways when you cross that intersection out in Decatur. When are they going to put a traffic light there!"

"I will," she said, and changed gears to back out of the driveway.

"Call us when you get there!" her mother called and waved from the sidewalk.

Jessie couldn't help but think of the last time she had been on the road from Athens—when Jack had driven her home for Carter's funeral. She adjusted the radio in search for more upbeat tunes. The closer to Athens she got, the more her spirit lightened and she was glad she'd accepted Jack's invitation. He had called the night before to be sure of what time she would arrive at the Lumpkin Street sorority house.

"My classes are over at eleven," he had said. "I'll meet you at the house for lunch." After Jessie had pledged Alpha Chi, Jack had become known by her sisters as the one who had come to her side when she received the news of Carter's death. He would always be welcome there.

Soon after she entered the Athens city limits, Jessie cruised down the hill on Baxter and glanced over at Creswell Dorm. The memory of her last day at the dorm washed over her as she passed it, but she brushed it off and continued to the corner. She waited to make a right onto Lumpkin and watched students moving at the street crossing from Sanford Stadium toward Bolton Cafeteria. The pre-game activities were well underway and red and black banners waved from every light pole up Lumpkin.

The downstairs door from the sorority parking lot swung open from the weight of her suitcase. The lights were on in the wood-paneled chapter room with decorations on long tables for the big weekend. She imagined her first chapter meeting inside once she returned to school and went through initiation.

She heard voices erupt from the kitchen. "Just in time for our TGIF lunch, Miss Jessie! We're setting up the buffet line right now."

Tom and Bonnie's warmhearted welcome was medicine for her, as it had been for all the Alpha Chi sisters over the years. The couple's commitment to everyone who passed through the halls of the house year after year was obvious. Tears welled in Jessie's eyes. She hadn't been in school long before Carter's death, yet they remembered her. "Lots of excitement this weekend on campus, Miss Jessie!" said Tom. "Living and dining rooms are all decorated for the alumni visits this weekend."

Jessie continued to the doorway to see red carnation bouquets on the dining tables and on the living room piano. She remembered the excitement of the sisters' dinner gatherings in the living room, where they sang the evening blessing. She thought of the first time she saw the president bring a candle from behind her back to start its passage among the sisters.

If a candle was blown out by a sister during the first round, it meant she had received a fraternity pin. After a second round, it meant that a sister was engaged. Bonnie and Tom often recounted the story of a special night, when a candle passed three times—and a sister had announced her elopement over the weekend!

"Let me help you with that bag, Miss Jessie," said Tom, emerging from the kitchen. "Most of the girls are still in class but Miss Linda told us you were coming. Shepherd's pie for dinner tonight!"

Jessie returned with him to the kitchen. "How about I just pull up a stool and talk to you and Bonnie while you finish there? I think you'll have a few extras today for lunch. My friend Jack is coming by."

Bonnie chuckled. "Mr. Jack? He's been here already this morning. I think he left something for you in the front hall."

The size of Jessie's grin could be matched only by her excitement. She bounced off the stool and hurried through the kitchen's swinging door to the black and white checkered tile hallway in the front of the house. There on the table at the mailroom was a purple package with a silver ribbon. She ripped open the note addressed to her, and her eyes brightened at the message. *I'm ready, if you are! Love, Jack.*

A large Northwest football jersey with the number 30 on the back was wrapped inside—Jack's number when he played safety on the high school team. She held the jersey in front of her at a nearby mirror and heard a familiar voice behind her.

"I can't wait to see it on you."

THE DOORBELL RANG AND MADELINE REYNOLDS opened the door to find a tall young soldier standing on the front step. He stood at attention, his shoulders straight, and then removed his service cap and placed it under his arm. "Excuse me, ma'am. Is this the home of Jessica Reynolds?"

Madeline smiled at the young man. "Yes, it is. I'm her mother."

"I'm sorry to stop by like this, ma'am. I'm Matthew Randall. I sent Jessica a letter awhile back."

Madeline thought for a moment. "Oh, yes. The letter about Carter." She stepped aside. "Won't you come in? I'm afraid Jessie's not here. She left for Athens earlier today."

He stepped inside and could instantly feel the home's warmth. "I didn't have a phone number for her," he said, "so I took a chance. I'm on temporary assignment here in Atlanta for a while…down at the recruitment center on Ponce de Leon.""

The scent of vanilla drifted from the kitchen. "I'm sorry you missed her," said Madeline. "I know your letter meant a lot to her." She paused. "Can I offer you something to drink…eat perhaps?"

"Thank you, ma'am, but I'll be on my way. It was nice to meet you."

"I'll be sure and tell her you stopped by," said Madeline.

"Yes, ma'am. Thank you." Matt walked back to his assigned military recruitment vehicle parked in front. He sat down behind the wheel and experienced an unexplained disappointment. He had fought the urge to find the directions to Longwood Drive, but Jessie's letter to him with her return address kept rising to the top of his duffel bag. He drove to the top of the street and stopped before turning onto Northside Drive and scolded himself. *What was I thinking!*

Sisters filtered their way through the large commercial kitchen and Tom and Bonnie greeted each one by name. Some had only short breaks between classes to stop by for lunch and all was ready—the self-serve buffet lunch menus were always carefully planned based on the girls' schedules. Jessie welcomed each of their their hugs while Jack sat on a stool next to her. He was encouraged to see her spirit rise with each embrace.

Linda soon appeared and wrapped her arms around her little sister. "We all have missed you."

"It *does* feel good to be back," said Jessie, remembering Reverend Hamilton's counsel. *Seeing your friends and being back in your school surroundings will help you move closer to recovery, Jessie.*

After lunch, Jessie joined Linda in her room to unpack. "Tom and Bonnie's lunches are way too good," said Jessie. "My scales would be screaming after a semester of their meals."

Linda nodded. "I would say Jack sure enjoyed lunch too. Word made the rounds that he dropped off a package for you this morning."

"Yeah, look. It's his Northwest jersey." Jessie held it up to herself again and looked in the mirror.

"Back home in Elberton, a jersey was the one thing we sometimes got before a senior ring," said Linda.

"I know. I cannot imagine what my life would be like without Jack." Jessie checked her makeup and hair in the mirror. "He said he had a fun afternoon planned."

She changed into shorts and her Alpha Chi t-shirt and looked at Linda. "It's good to be back."

SEVERAL GIRLS HAD GATHERED IN THE den TV room to watch the Friday afternoon soap operas while others mingled by the mailroom. On her way down the hall, Jessie saw still others in their rooms, packing their bags for the weekend. When she came down the back stairwell, she heard Jack's distinctive laugh from the TV room, and hurried to where he was.

"What's so funny?"

He shook his head. "I'm just amazed at the amount of luggage I see going out the door for the weekend...and it's only for one sister!"

Jessie peered outside and nodded her head with a smile. "Ah, yes, that has to be Mary Lou packing her car. She sets the packing standard for most of the sisters. I think she dates a guy from Clemson."

Jack's attention was all on her. "You look great! Ready for some fun?"

She grabbed her bag with her cutoffs and his jersey. "Absolutely! Lead the way!"

"Terry said to tell you hello and that he hopes to see you while you're here," said Jack. "It'll have to be after tomorrow's game, though. I think Coach Dooley will give everyone some playing time, even the freshmen and rising sophomores."

"I always knew that Terry would make it big," she said.

"Yeah," said Jack. "I remember hearing Coach talk about the Georgia recruiters calling him our junior year and checking Terry's stats."

They reached Jack's Volkswagen's and Jessie felt at home inside as they pulled out of the driveway onto Lumpkin. She marveled at Jack's animated gestures, all performed while he also shifted gears and smoothly make the turns around each curve. She had missed his enthusiasm.

They arrived at a grassy parking area above the Oconee River bluff. "I think I packed all we need," he said. "You want to carry the quilt?" She hesitated at the site of the folded patchwork throw on the seat which reminded her of the quilt that remained on her bed at home.

Jack threw towels over his shoulder and picked up a red cooler and a bag. He pointed to an opening in the large oaks that led to a sandy beach below some falls. Jessie gathered her bag and the quilt. "Hold on to me," he said. "This path can be slippery."

A few brothers were already there with large coolers and small portable grills. Firewood was stacked to one side near a rock formation. "I can tell *you've* been here before," said Jessie.

"Yeah, we come down mostly on weekend afternoons when the

weather's nice. The brothers call it the 'hole in the wall.' He pointed to the dam upstream.

"It's beautiful. Look at the old mill over there. I wish I could paint it."

"Maybe you will someday."

Jack placed his cooler to one side of the quilt he spread out for them to sit on. Jessie took his hand and sat down beside him. She closed her eyes and took a deep breath.

Jack looked at her, his eyes filled with anticipation. "Come on! Take off your shoes. The water isn't deep here." He reached for her hand and pulled her up beside him. They stepped through the flowing water across a stone path. They made their way back through friends splashing—much to the dismay of some of the girls, who had more concern for their outfits, hair and makeup.

Jessie thought of her childhood days, when she'd never shied away from playfulness. She tried to splash Jack but he dodged the water. He, on the other hand, caught her dead on.

She sputtered and Jack's laughter echoed across the beach. She laughed with him and beamed. "You got me!" And then she splashed him again.

After both were soaked, Jack grabbed her hand. "Let's take a break."

Jessie squeezed water from the ends of her hair. "I'm glad we came here," she said. "It feels like the Tiger's Den back home."

Jack reflected on their times together over the past year. "Funny how we somehow have so many moments on a river." He scratched his head. He wanted to say something meaningful about their journey, but a fraternity brother interrupted the moment and hollered a command for Jack to bring him a beer.

When he returned from the errand, he grumbled. "I'll be glad when initiation is over," he said. "Some of them can make it pretty tough on us pledges. We lucked up on the G-Day game this weekend. If it were like the games in the fall, the pledges would be assigned all kinds of things."

"Like what?" asked Jessie.

"Don't you remember last fall how we had to go early to all the games and block out seats for the fraternity in the student section?"

"Oh, yeah," she said. "I forgot about that."

Jack realized that the fall reference brought back painful memories and stoked the small campfire he had built in front of them. The sun was setting and a chill was settling through the evening air. Jessie pulled Jack's jersey from her bag to cover herself. He rubbed her shoulders and hands. "You're cold," he said.

She looked deep into his eyes and smiled. "I didn't bring the special gloves you gave me," she said.

His eyes brightened. "That's okay. You have me."

They sat on the quilt and Jessie pulled her knees up and wrapped her arms around them. He placed his arms around her and pulled the quilt up tight over her shoulders, leaning over to give her a kiss on the cheek.

Although part of Jessie wanted more, she changed the subject when she heard another of the brothers barking orders to a pledge. She'd heard rumors that there were sometimes harsh requirements to become a brother, including hazing.

"What else do they make you do?"

"Can't really talk about that, you know. One of those oath things." He stoked the fire again. "I need to add more firewood. And I'm hungry. How about you?"

"Sounds great. What can I do?" asked Jessie.

He smiled. "You're already doing it," he said.

Jack roasted hot dogs on a stick and took ketchup, mustard, and relish from the bag. It was the perfect supper. Jessie took a bite. "These are so good!" said Jessie.

Jack chuckled. "My parents taught me a lot about grilling, cooking... that sort of thing when I first worked at Mason's. I'm trying to keep it quiet with the brothers or next thing I know, I will be put on the line in the kitchen back at the house!"

Jessie took another bite and leaned in toward Jack. "What else can you cook?"

"I think maybe that should be a surprise. We'll go over to the lake house in Clayton sometime. I can cook you up quite a meal there."

"You've mentioned the lake house before, but I've never seen your aunt and uncle's place. And," she said, with a mischievous look, "I like surprises."

Jack drove much slower on the return to Athens and reached for Jessie's hand as they made their way back to the house. The front lawn was scattered with couples returning to the house for the evening and walking to the to the front door for their goodnights. The pledge trainer had gathered some of her charges out front to serenade the dates with *The Sweetheart Song.*

"It's good to be back, Jack," said Jessie. "I'm actually beginning to *feel* again."

Jack tried to think of something profound to say but was at a loss. "Tomorrow will be another good day. I have something special planned. That is, if the brothers will lighten up."

Jack wrapped the quilt tighter around her shoulders and Jessie's thoughts wandered. Was Jack doing all this because of his promise to Carter? Or was it more? They had parked in the lower lot behind the house with only the light from the moon and stars. "Can we sit here a while longer?"

"Sure," he said. He pulled Jessie close and kissed her forehead, neck, and then lips. Her heart was overwhelmed with the love she felt that night.

"Today was so perfect, Jack."

Linda was waiting in her room when Jessie finally went in. "The shoals are nice this time of year," she said. "How was it?"

"It was fun. Jack's always been a good friend, but he's beginning to be more than that."

"What do you mean?"

"I know there are girls who would jump at a chance to have his attention. A little saying between us recently has been 'Are you ready for this?'" Jessie motioned with her hand between herself and an imaginary Jack.

"And what's your answer, Jessie? From what I can tell and from what I know from our conversations, his attention is all yours. Jack's a great guy. Just be careful with your heart," she said, pausing. "And his, too."

JESSIE AWOKE TO A BEAUTIFUL SUNNY morning and the sounds of hair dryers and the chatter of sisters dressing for their dates. She sat up and stretched. Linda stood looking out the window. "I'm wearing a short-sleeved dress for the game today," she said. "How about you?"

"I brought a dress that should work. It *does* get hot in the student section with people packed in tight."

Linda raised the window and the sounds of music echoed across campus. The drums of the Redcoat Band reverberated in the distance. Cars flowed up and down Lumpkin and the parking lot across the street at Myers complex was already full.

"We've got the best sorority location," said Linda. "Right on campus and up the street from the stadium. The pledges are already outside guarding our parking lot and holding up posters for the alums." Jessie joined her at the window and wished she could join the pledges, but she couldn't—her inactive status kept her inside.

The room intercom came on. "Bonnie says the breakfast line is ready in the kitchen."

Jessie shook her head and smiled. "They are too good to be true."

"Come on," said Linda. "You know it will be a spread!"

The girls took the back stairs to the kitchen for easy access without being seen by visitors who had arrived early in the front. Tom and Bonnie were busy making their way back and forth, setting the tables in the dining room with the game-day refreshments for the alums.

"Mother Mac," the Alpha Chi housemother, took her position in the entry hall to welcome the guests. Her quarters were adjacent to the lobby and den/TV room. Older alumni had filled her small living room with their purses and jackets until it was time to walk to the stadium.

Linda slipped through the lobby with Jessie and up to Mother Mac to remind her that Jessie was there. "Now, Jessie," she said, "we're looking forward to you being back with us real soon."

"Yes, ma'am," said Jessie. "I am too."

Mother Mac gave her a hug and signaled to Linda. "Don't forget to check the cooler in the kitchen. Tom and Bonnie made extra banana cake for you girls this weekend."

Once breakfast was done, Jessie and Linda went back upstairs. The feeling that she was home was all Jessie could think of as she finished dressing. When a sister buzzed in to tell her that Jack had arrived, Jessie's heart skipped a beat, and she grabbed her purse and checked her makeup one last time.

Jack was waiting next to the foyer's main staircase dressed in a suit and tie. Jessie came down the back way and sneaked up on him.

"I thought you might be coming down these stairs," he said.

"Not yet. After I'm initiated. Only sisters are allowed to use it."

Jack looked up at the grand staircase and knew there was more to learn about the ins and outs of pledges versus sisters at the sorority. He turned back to her. "You look nice," he said, and held out his hand. Jessie took it and the two headed down the few steps to the front door.

"I was going to say the same about you! The last time I saw you in a suit and tie was…"

Jack froze for a second, afraid Jessie was thinking of the suit he'd worn for Carter's funeral, but he was quick to recover. "New Year's Eve at Cherokee."

Her face brightened. "Yes, you're right!"

JESSIE EXPECTED THEY WOULD WALK DOWN Lumpkin and over the bridge to the stadium, but instead, smiling from ear to ear, Jack steered her toward his car. "We have a few stops before the game." She raised her eyebrows, questioning. "Don't worry," he said. "We've got time."

They headed down Lumpkin and passed the people lined up for tailgating orders out the doors of Stan's Sandwich Shop. Red and black tents were set up outside Clark Howell with students and alums tailgating on every parking spot and knoll. The spaces around Oglethorpe and Boggs Halls were the same—down to the packed parking lots facing the stadium. "Look. There's the Bulldog RV. That family from Greenville never misses a game."

Jack drove on past the stadium. Thousands of students and guests made their way to the entry on the west. A turn up toward North Campus past LeConte Hall brought back Jessie's not so pleasant memories of her first period political science class.

She couldn't stand the mystery any longer. "Where are we going?"

"Hold on. Hold on." Jack took a left up the hill and pulled in the parking area behind the Art Building. A few alums were there in claimed spots, setting up chairs and tables with food containers waiting to be opened for lunch.

Jessie looked over at Jack. "What are we doing *here?*"

"Come on," he said and grabbed a basket from behind his seat.

Jessie took his hand, and they entered the building. Art pieces were displayed on every wall and pedestal. They passed a room down the hallway, and she heard a familiar voice. "Jessica!"

Jessie's mouth dropped open. "Mr. Baker?" It had been almost a year since graduation and seeing one of her favorite Northwest teachers was a definite surprise. She and Jack sat together in his classes.

"I asked Jack if maybe you two could interact with some of our junior and senior art students from Northwest. They are considering attending here and we are visiting with some of their parents."

Jessie looked around in shock and Jack placed his arm around her. The students listened attentively to Jack and Jessie banter about their days in art class together, the district art competitions, and their first-year college experiences.

When all was done, Mr. Baker thanked them. "That was impressive, you two. I think your interaction gives them a good introduction to campus life and the art scene here."

In an adjacent room were tables and chairs set up to allow for tailgating baskets brought by the families. The faculty had provided a nice spread of Georgia-themed desserts. Jack pulled his chair closer to Jessie's and opened his basket.

"I hope you were okay with this. When I was home for a break and went to see Coach, I ran into Mr. Baker. It just kind of came together."

Mr. Baker walked over to join them. "You two always had an eye for art. I wondered if you would continue it somehow." Jessie thought of her sketch book sitting unopened for months on her bedroom desk. He headed to speak to one of the visiting families.

"Mr. Baker?" called Jessie. He turned back to face her. "I wanted to thank you for something you said several years ago. You know, the 'make it about others' you suggested for our junior class Christmas project."

"You remember that?"

"How could I forget it? I hear it calling me all the time." Jack leaned her way to show his agreement.

"Then listen to it," said Mr. Baker. "Listen to it—you've remembered it for a reason."

Chapter 15

Early Sunday morning, Stephen stepped out on the porch of the farmhouse. It felt strange not to be rushing to dress and prepare for Sunday services. He carried the coffee cup that had spoken to him from the kitchen counter—the fresh ground coffee was like none other he'd ever tasted. He took a sip and squinted as he looked to the east to see the sun over the horizon. It was the first time in years he had slept in.

The cane fishing pole was still propped next to the door. He tried to remember the last time he'd gone fishing when he heard a voice.

"Morning!"

"Good morning!"

"You can call me Comfort. I didn't want to disturb you when you arrived yesterday evening. Thought you needed some time to yourself."

Stephen walked to the edge of the porch and extended his hand. "Nice to meet you, Comfort. I went to bed early and never slept so well."

The older man's eyes crinkled when he smiled. "The ole rooster sometimes interrupts that." He pointed a pair of pruning shears toward the garden behind him. "I like to tend the roses in the morning," he said. "I'll be taking care of things around here for you during your stay. I stay in the cabin just down the road there."

"Can I get you a cup of coffee?"

"Maybe some other time. Sunday morning, you know. Got to get myself ready for church." Comfort closed the garden gate and waved. "I'll be 'round if you need anything." He disappeared out of sight down the dirt and gravel driveway.

THE G-DAY FESTIVITIES OVER, THE QUADRANGLE behind Myers Hall was quiet. Jack and Jessie had met for an early Sunday breakfast.

"Wanta go for a walk?" asked Jack.

Jessie nodded and they headed for the quad. They crossed the stadium bridge and she pointed to the empty field below. "Seeing Terry play in the game yesterday was so exciting."

Jack smiled. "I'm glad the Red Team won. Terry is working hard to make first string next season." He squeezed her hand and thought of how good it felt. He hoped she was as happy as he was that she was by his side. Not even the harassment by some brothers at the game had rained on his contentment.

Jessie squeezed back. "It was a nice surprise to see Mr. Baker yesterday. His idea for his students coming here to visit was a good one." They walked a few more steps, enjoying the quiet. "We were lucky to have some pretty amazing teachers at Northwest, Jack. Mr. Baker, Mrs. Laney, Coach. I hope I can be an encouragement to students like them some day."

"Well, you're in the right place. You have always had a way with children, Jess, and you know the Education Department here is one of the best."

"You think you'll stay with your idea of majoring in business?" she asked him.

Jack nodded. "Definitely. It is the most practical thing for me. At some point I'll watch for the right internship to know for sure."

"No thought of taking over the family business?"

He shook his head. "Mason's is great, and I may play a role in it someday, but not likely as a short order cook. I'm proud of it and all, but Dad's typical line is 'Get yourself an education that doesn't require you to work seven days a week with no vacation.'" Jessie nodded and he continued. "Even with providing a good life for our family, the restaurant world can be brutal."

They strolled along, comfortably silent for a moment before Jessie spoke again. "Will you work with Coach this summer again at his camp?"

Jack shrugged his shoulders. "Not sure yet. I need to see him again about that. Maybe next weekend. I'll try to get on the road early and catch him after classes on Friday. How about you? What will you do this summer?"

"I need to start looking. My parents have been patient with me, but I keep hearing gentle hints that I should start searching for something to help my focus. Especially until I come back to school."

They turned toward Lumpkin Street and the sorority house. "I guess you'll head back home today," said Jack.

Jessie nodded. "Will I see you when you come home?"

He stopped at the bridge and wrapped his arms around her. With a gentle kiss, he looked into her eyes and said, "You can count on it!"

COMFORT WIPED HIS HANDS AND CHECKED the clock on his kitchen stove. He had just enough time to clean up and make it to church before the children arrived. His dress shirt hung on the closet door handle. He slipped it on and buttoned it and then combed his hair with his fingers.

He ran his hand across his kitchen table—the first table his father taught him to make. Miss Elizabeth had given wooden blocks he'd made for a children's Christmas art project to their parents to take home and he'd made more. The different block sizes were perfect for her painted nativity patterned characters and animals. Comfort had built a wooden stable for each child to house their projects. He smiled. More and more parents were sending their children to the church due to Elizabeth's reputation.

He checked again to see if he had everything, and then remembered the animals he had carved for Miss Elizabeth's preschool class—two horses like the ones in his care across the pasture. They were polished and ready to add to Noah's ark.

MATT POURED A SECOND CUP OF coffee. Watching the sunrise had become a special Atlanta morning tradition for him—the view from his apartment balcony was perfect. He sat in silence on a bar stool perch.

He glanced toward the closed door of his spare bedroom. Starr had come in late the previous night—Perry Michaels had booked her for several shows at a tavern on North Highland. He knew Starr loved pastries, so he'd made a special stop at Highland Bakery the afternoon before. He stepped in from the balcony and placed the box out on the kitchen counter.

He returned to his perch and thought about his unannounced visit to Jessica Reynold's. It had been a mistake in his mind, and he didn't want Starr to press him again on taking time for a personal life, so he hadn't told her about it.

"Morning."

Matt turned to see Starr standing in the doorway with her arms wrapped around herself. She beamed. "Does that Highland Bakery box have what I think it has in it?!"

"You got it. Bear claws, cinnamon buns…I even had them add some of their famous coconut macaroons!" He took another sip of coffee and walked back inside with her.

Starr grabbed a napkin. "Who could ask for a better brother! You are going to make someone the best husband someday." Matt was silent. She pulled out the bar stool at the counter and bit into a cinnamon bun and waited for his response. "Okay. Here you go again. Don't be like Dad and shut me out."

"Not hardly. But I know I *am* like him when it comes to my commitment to the military. I have come to terms with the fact that some things require a sacrifice." He reached over to pinch a bite off Starr's sweet roll. "And…I have to say, just like *others of us* also have come to terms with their sacrifices, too."

"Okay, okay. You're right. My career has taken its own toll on my personal life. But I have high hopes for that to change one of these days. And you should too."

COACH WOKE EARLY AND PICKED UP the Sunday newspaper from the front walkway. He wandered to his home office and shuffled through papers on his desk for a brochure he'd gotten a few months before. "Where is it?" he said out loud, as if there were someone there to help him find it. "I know I put it somewhere here."

He'd kept the brochure because of the conversation with the principal…and the art teacher at Northwest. He'd run into John Baker in the faculty lounge the same afternoon he had visited Principal Kelley's office.

"I just met with the boss," he'd told the art teacher. "Kind of strange. Ever since Stephen Hamilton told me about his sabbatical, the idea of it won't let me go."

"I heard about that," said John. "Sounds like a real gift. I have had Italy on the top of my bucket list. You know, where I could go and paint. Ahhh...the streets and shops on the Sorrento waterfront!"

"Hmmm, Italy. I don't know. I can't put my finger on a place or something I would want to do. But, like I said, the idea of it won't let me go." The two pulled up chairs to the break table. "I told Kelley that I would not be hosting my usual sports camp at the school this summer."

"Oh? No sports camp? That will be the first time in how many years, Paul?"

"Many years for sure, and I have no clue what I am going to do. I just know it needs to be something else. A change. It's time for a change."

SHERIFF BRYAN PULLED INTO THE CHURCH parking lot and watched children skip down the sidewalk toward him, their parents not far behind. A truck pulled in and parked close to the building. The children waved to their teacher and shouted her name. "Miss Elizabeth!"

Elizabeth opened the church door and greeted each child by name as he or she went by. Nothing matched her love of seeing the extended joy and wonder in their eyes through their church experience. Elizabeth's appreciation of nature and God's creation was as present in her lesson plans at school as in her church classroom.

"What happy faces this morning!" she exclaimed. "See if you can find the surprise in our room." The children ran past her with delight.

Sheriff Bryan took one more official look around the church parking lot and straightened his tie. This Sunday, the circuit pastor would preach at another county church and the parishioners would take responsibility themselves for services. Because Elizabeth's program with the children was attracting more families, the members had asked the conference for a minister to come more often.

"Looks like you are going to have another room full this morning, Elizabeth," said Yates.

"I hope so," she answered. "I'll need your help again with the snack break."

Elizabeth took every opportunity to provide healthy snacks for the children of the community. She and Jeb had even positioned a basket with fruit at The Mercantile and at the adjacent Garden Shop for young visitors. Elizabeth had noticed children making more frequent visits to the fruit basket—she had brought their obvious hunger to the attention of the local city council on more than one occasion.

The children needed no parental escorts to their Sunday school room. Some stopped along the way to visit their own artwork, carefully placed on bulletin boards outside the doorway. But most raced to see the large table at the room's entry where Elizabeth had placed Comfort's handcrafted ark. The children could easily find the new addition since the previous Sunday. "I see it!" said one child. "There they are! Horses!" shouted another child. Small batches of hay and oats were found on the table. Comfort had added a bridle from the farm's stable tack room. He stood over at the triple row of windows inside and smiled as he watched their discovery.

"Yes," said Miss Elizabeth when joining them. "And Mr. Comfort is here today to talk to you about the horses he cares for."

Sheriff Bryan walked by the classroom door and peeked in to see Comfort surrounded by the children. Elizabeth, leaning against the door, smiled at the sheriff. "The children do love him so," she said. "It's like he can't do enough for them."

Yates nodded in agreement. The two knew more than enough about Comfort's unusual commitment to the town's children. He watched the children move the wooden animals up the ramp of the ark and position the pairs two by two. "The Randall's have a guest out at the farmhouse. Thought I'd stop by for an introduction."

Elizabeth glanced at him and back at the children. "It's been a while since I've seen Christine and her children. Wonder how she's doing?"

"Comfort said the Randalls were in town at the farm for the holidays, but I never saw them. Not once," replied Yates.

"Doesn't seem fair that things ended the way they did for her with Mitch. She and her family have always had the best hearts of anyone I know," said Elizabeth. "Jeb has offered to help them over the years, but she wouldn't accept his offer. I know Comfort has made a difference to keep up the farm. They let us board our horses at the farm now."

Yates glanced over at Comfort playing with the children. "He will never forget what he owes that family."

Jessie reflected on the weekend on her way home. The thought of Jack's final kiss made her smile. She thought about Linda's advice during their heart-to-heart talk. She could not imagine doing anything that would not protect Jack's heart.

The surprise meeting with Mr. Baker and his students had also made a big impression on her. The importance of her education and her dream of being a teacher had regained a place of purpose in her thoughts. Mr. Baker's encouragement to continue to listen to her heart in "making it about others" was a reminder she could not forget.

Jessie thought too about Sgt. Randall's letter. The letter and her walk in the park after she'd read it had brought her an indescribable peace. She pulled the car into her driveway and leaned over to grab her purse. In her haste, the items in the purse fell out onto the floor, including the "One Day at a Time" medallion Carter had left for her. She took a deep breath and slipped the medallion back into her purse.

The quilt Jack had given her at their outing at the shoals lay across the back seat and she thought of their special evening together and the summer plans the two had discussed. The picture of the beautiful waterfall returned to her mind and the sketch pad on her desk that had not been opened in months.

Ladd bounded out of the house to meet her. "Hey, honey. How was your weekend?"

"It was good!" she said, and then paused. "I've been thinking, Dad," she said. "I need to look for a summer job."

"Perhaps Mrs. Riley might have some work for you again. I know she wanted to make up for that Allen Monroe and Marcus Jacobs assignment catastrophe last year."

"Maybe. Remind me to tell you and Mom about seeing Mr. Baker and some of his students at the Art Building this weekend. But first I have a phone call to make."

Ladd reached for his daughter's suitcase. Jessie grabbed Jack's quilt from the back seat and ran into the house and up the stairs. She knew Reverend Hamilton might be difficult to contact, but he had left a number where he could be reached.

Chapter 16

Stephen was in the kitchen preparing his lunch when he heard a knock on the door. He wiped his hands and headed to the front door, thinking it might be Comfort. But a man he'd not seen was standing on the porch.

"Afternoon," said the man. "I'm Sheriff Bryan." The sheriff looked Stephen up and down.

"Hello," said Stephen. "Won't you come in?"

"Nope. Just checking on things here," said the sheriff. "I have business to attend to." Yates looked inside the doorway and back out to the front porch. "You have business in these parts?"

Stephen wondered what the sheriff was thinking, but due to the gruffness of the man, he was unwilling at this point to be overly forthcoming. "I am taking a bit of an extended vacation, you might say."

"Not much of a vacation spot for most folks." Sheriff Bryan glanced at the license plate on Stephen's car and made a mental note. "Well, then. I best be getting to my rounds." He patted his revolver and turned to go back to his cruiser with not so much as a tip of his hat.

Stephen stepped back through the doorway. "Thanks for stopping by," he said. The cruiser churned on the gravel drive as the officer left the yard. Stephen watched as a cloud of dust obscured the vehicle as it proceeded down the driveway. When it was finally out of sight, he returned to the kitchen and finished making his lunch. While he ate, he decided it was time for him to venture into town to get a lay of the land and meet some of the other people of Cross Hill.

Just then, the phone in the farmhouse rang.

"Rev. Hamilton?"

"Jessie!"

"I know I shouldn't be bothering you, but I put the number for where you'd be in South Carolina in my address book. You are the only one I can talk to."

"You're not bothering me at all." Stephen looked at the communion set on the table in front of him. He already missed hearing from his Atlanta friends and the sound of Jessie's voice warmed him. He sat back in his chair.

The reverend described his surroundings to her and told her how he wished she could see it and create one of her paintings of the landscape. She told him of her afternoon with Jack at Barrett Shoals and the beautiful image of the old mill cascading waterfall and what it had been like to return to the college campus. She realized while talking that she'd experienced a breath of new life.

After the phone call, Jessie went back downstairs to the den where her mother was sitting. She told her about her visit with Jack, seeing her sorority sisters, the G-Day game and the encounter with Mr. Baker.

"Oh," said Madeline suddenly, "I almost forgot. That sergeant who wrote you the letter about Carter came by."

"Really?" said Jessie, caught off guard. She sat down on the piano bench across from her mother. "I thought he was at Fort Benning."

"He didn't say much after I told him you weren't here, but he did say something about being on assignment at the recruitment center over on Ponce de Leon. Maybe you'll hear from him again."

Jessie shrugged. "It was probably just a courtesy, I'm sure." But she was curious that the young sergeant would make such a visit. "He didn't say anything else?" she asked.

Their conversation was interrupted when Jessie heard the humming of an Irish lullaby from the hallway. Her father appeared in the doorway. "I put your suitcase upstairs."

"Thanks, Dad."

Ladd came into the den and sat down next to his wife.

"Dad, did you meet Sergeant Randall when he came by?"

"No, and frankly, I was a bit surprised when your mother told me about it."

Jessie frowned. "Why?"

"These days the military is going through a lot with folks criticizing their every move. When your mother told me, I decided it was just a nice gesture—as was his letter."

Madeline interrupted. "Tell us more about your visit in Athens."

Jessie sat back and thought for a moment. "Well, I loved seeing Jack and Mr. Baker. That was a big surprise. And the girls at the house gave me a lot to look forward to when I return to school next fall."

She felt the medallion in her pocket. "When I came home I called Reverend Hamilton—to hear his voice and about where he is. He said we are both following new paths." She looked at her father. "Like I said, Dad, I'm going to start checking out some summer job possibilities tomorrow. It's time."

Jessie went upstairs to unpack her suitcase and sat down on her bed. She pulled out Jack's jersey from the top of her tote—the weekend with him had renewed her spirit. Their time at the shoals brought a smile to her face and she reached for the sketch pad which had sat unopened for so long. She began a sketch of the mill and waterfall when the phone next to her bedside rang. She hugged the receiver under her chin to answer and continued to sketch. "Hello?"

"Jessie?" said a familiar voice.

"Sandy! Is that you?" Jessie was thrilled to hear from the friend she'd shared afternoons riding her horse at Chastain Park and so many other good times during high school. "I'm sorry we didn't get to talk much at the New Year's party. How's school in Knoxville?"

"It's good. I thought I would try to reach you before I went back."

"You're home now? Can you come by before you head back? I would love to see you."

"I wish I could but I've got to get on the road." Sandy was silent. "I heard you were in Athens this weekend. I guess you saw Jack?"

"Yes, I did. It was great."

Another period of silence. "I had wanted to see you...well, talk to you...about Jack."

"Really?"

"Yeah. Maybe he told you. I asked him to come to Knoxville for our big UT Volunteers weekend."

"No. He must have forgotten." A strange feeling went through Jessie as the conversation continued. "I did see him," she said cheerfully. "And Mr. Baker too. He was there with some students from Northwest who are interested in the art department."

"Jack told me he couldn't come and had something going on that weekend."

"Maybe it's something with his fraternity," said Jessie in his defense. "You know he's going through pledging and initiation is coming up."

Sandy paused again. "Jess, we've been good friends forever. I hope you will understand."

"Understand what?"

"I have to ask you. When are you going to let him go?"

"Let him go? Jack? What do you mean?"

"You know what I mean. You two have been friends forever and he will always be there for you with Carter gone. But he's never going to look at anyone else unless you move on."

Jessie was baffled. "I never knew that you thought of Jack as more than a friend."

"That's because Jack was always at your side," said Sandy. "And it's not just me. There are plenty of girls who would love to date him."

"I don't know what to say."

"You know you can't tell him about this conversation, right, Jessie?"

Jessie looked down at her sketch pad. The delight she'd felt at the memory of their time at the falls had now morphed into confusion.

"Jessie?" Sandy repeated.

"Right...I wouldn't."

Jessie hung up the phone and slumped onto her bed. As life seemed to be taking a positive turn, she faced a reality she had never even considered. She opened the bedside table and pulled out the letter from Sgt. Randall and read it again.

Chapter 17

The bell on the Mercantile door rang and Jeb looked up from the shelf he was stocking. "Hey there," he said to the stranger.

"Good afternoon," said Stephen. "Nice store you have here."

"Been in the family for years. What can I do for you?"

"Just a few groceries. Eggs?"

Jeb pointed toward the back of the store. "We have farm fresh ones over there. Local butter, dairy, anything you need."

Stephen moved through the aisles looking for ingredients for his meals for the next week. He heard the bell on the door ring again announcing the entrance of another.

"Sis!" hollered Jeb. "School out late?"

"There was a faculty meeting today. It ran long. The faculty all agreed this afternoon that we've got to come up with a plan for the children this summer. And not just activities and structure. They need good food."

"I knew the county had raised the budget for more free lunches during the school year," answered Jeb.

Stephen walked from behind the shelving. "Oh!" exclaimed Elizabeth. "I didn't know we had a customer."

Jeb turned to Stephen. "Did you find what you're looking for? We have some fresh baked bread up front here. By the way, I'm Jeb Satterfield. This is my sister, Elizabeth."

"Nice to meet you. I'm Stephen Hamilton. I'm staying down at the Chapman farm." He placed several items on the counter.

Elizabeth smiled at the stranger and extended her hand. His clean-shaven face, lean frame and wrinkle-free clothes set him apart from the mill workers and farmers usually in their store. Stephen held her hand perhaps longer than most would have in an initial introduction and Jeb took notice.

"I'll take these things and a loaf of your bread," said Stephen finally. "No, make that two."

"Sure thing," said Jeb. "It's hunting season. The Chapmans allow hunters to stay at the farm when they're not in their deer stands."

Stephen smiled. "I'm more the fishing type," he said. "I hear the lake is well-stocked."

"Then you'll be needing some lures and bait," said Elizabeth. "We're waiting on more bait. The weekend and all. Sold out. But we'll have more soon."

Jeb looked around for the lures and fishing line on the shelf behind him and grabbed a package of each. "Here. On the house. You know, first time customer and all."

"I appreciate it," said Stephen. He smiled at Elizabeth, and pulled a couple of bills from his wallet and gave them to Jeb. Elizabeth averted her gaze, reaching for a paper sack for his groceries.

Jeb looked at the cash. "You gonna be here long? I can start you an account."

"No need," said Stephen. "And keep the change." He glanced back at Elizabeth. "Perhaps you can use it to start a food fund for the children."

Stephen exited and Jeb turned to Elizabeth. "Nice guy," he said.

"Uh, huh. Yes. Very nice." She made her way over to the window, pretending to dust off the shelves.

On his way to the car, Stephen glanced at the garden shop next door. He would stop there on his next visit to town, but he had a mission—to learn more about Camp Greenwood. The dilapidated sign had been on his mind since the day he'd arrived.

He made a trip back to the farmhouse to drop off his groceries and found Comfort on his cabin porch.

"I've been seeing to the horses. Just taking a rest."

Stephen reached in the bag and pulled out one loaf of bread and handed it to the caretaker. "I brought this for you from The Mercantile. The Satterfields said it is fresh baked here locally."

Comfort wiped his hands on his overalls and accepted the loaf. "Thanks."

"We haven't had a chance to get acquainted. I have an errand to run. How about a tour of the farm when I get back?"

Comfort nodded and nestled the loaf under his arm. "A tour this afternoon will be fine. Thank you for the bread. I'll go and make myself a sandwich for lunch right now."

"Sounds good," said Stephen. "I'm heading out now toward Greenwood. I saw a sign for a camp near there on my way here last week."

"Camp Greenwood? You going there?"

"Yes. I thought I would make a stop and check it out. You know anything about it?"

Comfort smiled. "It's a special place. Yes, sir, a very special place. I try to go there when I can. Tell Mr. Charles I'll be seeing him soon."

"Mr. Charles?"

"The director. Been there a long, long time."

"Come in," said the director, extending his hand. "Abbott Charles. Always happy to welcome a visitor. What brings you to our camp?" His hand and palms were rough with age, wear and tear.

"I'm Stephen Hamilton. I had passed on my way to Cross Hill several days ago and saw your sign," said Stephen. "Something told me I needed to pay a visit while I was in the area. Oh, and Comfort said to tell you he would see you soon."

"You mean ole Roy Jasper," said Abbott. He was silent for a moment. "Yes, many call him Comfort. He comes here almost every week. Brings us all kinds of things for the camp. He is quite a craftsman. Even collects things from other folks." He pointed to the bookshelves behind him. "Those baskets here for instance. Made by his great-aunt in Charleston."

Having been to Charleston, Stephen recognized the vintage sweet grass baskets. "I guess he inherited the family's crafting skills with his woodworking and carvings." He examined the variety of Comfort's work— from bookends to candlesticks, bread bowls and more. "He is very gifted."

Abbott touched one candlestick. "Yes, he has quite a story, that Roy. Not many know it."

Stephen wandered over to a literature stand and picked up a brochure about the camp.

"Would you like a tour?" Abbott asked. "We've been here a long time… as you can probably tell by the age of those cabins. I keep hoping for a way to keep us afloat, but these are challenging times. My time is soon coming to an end and the camp needs a new identity. A new direction."

Chapter 18

Early spring found college students coming home on the weekends to look for summer jobs. When Coach O'Connor heard Jack would be in town for a weekend visit, he called and asked him to stop by.

Jack entered the familiar Northwest hallway leading to the coach's office and stopped to gaze at the framed letterman jacket above the boys' locker room doorway. Those entering or leaving were reminded of the importance of strength and courage as they faced the challenges of the outside world. Coach stepped up beside him. "He's still with us in many ways," he said.

Jack nodded. "Carter was a good friend. I won't forget his sacrifice."

They stepped inside the office and Coach motioned toward the chair across from his desk. "Have a seat, Jack. You about ready for a summer break?"

"Yes, sir. I'm here to look for a job. You mentioned possibly a position here with you?"

"As it turns out, maybe not here."

Coach rubbed his hand across his forehead. "I got a call from Stephen Hamilton up in South Carolina. He's doing well and wanted to tell me about a camp up there needing some help. It may not have my name on it, but for some reason, I can't let go of the idea of a change from my summer routine here at school."

Jack was obviously disappointed. "Oh. I was hoping my summer job could be here with you."

"That's the thing, Jack. Stephen says the camp needs a lot of help. He met the director who has been there a long time and the camp is struggling. He asked if I would be interested in giving it a look, at least for the summer. If it's what I think it is, I'm wondering if you would consider coming with me as my summer assistant."

Jack's thoughts immediately turned to Jessie and his hopes of spending time with her. He had never considered anything other than being with her before they both returned to Athens in the fall. "I'm not sure about that, Coach. Just had it in my mind I would be working here at home this summer."

"It could be an opportunity to try something new and a change of scenery," said the coach. "Stephen is staying on a farm near there for his sabbatical."

"I need to think about it, Coach. Can I get back to you? When will you know about it for sure?"

"Soon. From the sound of it, I think it is just what *I've* been looking for. A change from the city and a change from school. Still working with young people at a camp with an opportunity to put my sports touch on it. Don't make a decision just yet—I'll be going up for a visit this weekend. I'll let you know what I think when I get back."

COMFORT HEARD THE CAR DRIVE UP to his cabin and pulled back the curtain to see Stephen stepping from his car. He didn't want to disappoint Miss Christine by not being a good host to her guest, so he picked up his jacket and greeted Stephen on the front porch. "Find the camp okay?"

"Yes. And just as you said, I met Mr. Charles. How fortunate to have such a property to benefit the children from around here."

"It was my home away from home for many years. Wish I could say it was in better shape."

Stephen looked toward a building behind the cabin. A power line ran to the outside. Timber and other materials were stacked neatly under an attached shed. Comfort followed his eyes. He was glad that the minister had not pried him with many questions about himself.

"I saw all your wood crafts at the camp," said Stephen. "The items in the farmhouse too. How I wish I had such a skill."

Comfort shrugged. "Us Jaspers lived off this land for decades and I used to help my Pa find wood and other materials for the making. He and Mr. Chapman helped me find my way and learn to do the same." He quickly changed the subject from himself. "You ready for that tour?"

"Sure. I've been looking forward to it."

Comfort pointed across the horses in the pasture then toward his truck. "Saddle up or shotgun?"

Stephen looked at the horses and chuckled. "I think I better call shotgun today."

They climbed into Comfort's old pickup. "She's not much these days," he said, "but she gets me where I need to be. And she's paid for… and can carry ten hay bales if I stack 'em right." He took the left fork toward the lake and the horses raced up to the fence. He tapped his horn and winked at Stephen, pointing to a black mare. "That one there is in charge." The horses tossed their heads and galloped along the fence line to the corner turn.

The frame of the truck jostled along the rugged dirt road. Stephen rested his arm on the truck's open window and looked at the landscape. A wooden dock appeared at the lake's edge. Comfort slowed to a stop and Stephen leaned forward to get a better view. "That's some fishing pond," he said.

"Best place in the county to try out that fishing pole on your porch," answered Comfort. The horses sounded their displeasure at being ignored. Comfort laughed. "They're spoiled."

"The lake is beautiful. Mind if we get out and take a look?" asked Stephen.

"Not at all," said Comfort. They walked down to the dock and Stephen spied a wooden cross to one side. The sabbatical had brought him an appreciation for the simple life, but he missed the people connections that fed him.

Comfort followed his gaze. "A reminder that the Lord is always with us, don't you know?"

Stephen stared at the cross in silence and Comfort sensed his guest might otherwise have less of a faith than his until Stephen said, "It *is* a nice reminder for me and all of us. I haven't been here long, Comfort, but this farm is a true gift. A way that God can speak to us in more ways than one." He paused. "I need to share with you what brought me here."

Stephen's confession was interrupted by the appearance of a cloud of dust on the gravel road to the lake. Comfort turned his attention to the vehicle when it made its way toward them and waved. "It's Miss Elizabeth! Don't usually see her 'cept on weekends."

She pulled up and came to an idling stop. Comfort trotted over to her car.

"Hi, Comfort," she said. "I saw your truck down here." She looked over at Stephen and held up a tin can. "And I brought you that bait we said we would get in at The Mercantile."

Comfort looked between the two and Elizabeth continued. "You *did* say you were more the fishing type rather than hunting."

"Oh, yes. Thanks," said Stephen. "Definitely more the fishing type."

Comfort could see the gleam in Elizabeth's eyes and Stephen's as well. "I was just showing our guest around the farm, Miss Elizabeth." He turned to Stephen. "Miss Elizabeth knows this farm as good as anyone. She's spent a lot of time over here."

Elizabeth smiled. "Well, thanks to you, Comfort, this place is what it is today."

Comfort looked at the two again. "I just remembered I have a delivery to make, Miss Elizabeth. Why don't you take Mr. Hamilton on the rest of the tour?"

She looked at Stephen. "I'd be glad to...if that's okay with you, Mr. Hamilton."

"Stephen. Call me Stephen."

Before Comfort could reach his truck, Stephen yelled. "Hey, Comfort! How about dinner tonight?" He held up the bait from Elizabeth and laughed. "Maybe a fish dinner!" Comfort gave him a thumbs-up and pulled away to his pretend errand.

"He's as dependable as they come," Elizabeth said, then turned and surveyed the lake. "If only these waters and the land could talk."

Stephen heard a sense of sadness in her tone. "I'm sure the farm has a rich history."

Elizabeth gestured to her car. "Let's drive up toward the north end."

The drive seemed endless. Along the way, Elizabeth pointed toward a grove of pecan trees, a well-maintained fence line, and finally a cabin bordered by corn and sunflower fields. She stopped the car and smiled at Stephen. "Now if you're into hunting, this is the place to come!"

"Is this still Chapman property?" he asked.

"Yep. There's more."

The gravel and dirt road ended, and she continued along a two-track lane with a grass median. At the road's end was a large circle groove. "Back here is the family cemetery. I don't get back here much. Comfort takes the horses here, though…on their exercises."

Stephen looked her way and then at the cemetery nearby. He could see that the fenced area was respectfully maintained and noted the family's final resting place. "I appreciate this tour. I have not met any of the Chapman family to thank them for my time here."

"You mean the Randalls," said Elizabeth. "There aren't any Chapmans left. Just Christine Randall and her children. She was a Chapman."

"Randall?"

"Yes. She's divorced, though. Comes every so often—mostly when she can connect with her children, Starr and Matt. Comfort sees to it that this place is always well-kept."

Stephen glanced again at the cemetery. "I would like to hear more. Why don't you join me and Comfort for dinner tonight?"

"I wouldn't want to intrude," she said.

"The more the merrier," replied Stephen.

Elizabeth nodded. "Okay, then. But only if you let me bring something."

"All right, then. By the way, I have come to have a major liking of that fresh bread from your store."

"Done!" said Elizabeth. "A bottle of our wine too…if that's okay."

Elizabeth dropped Stephen at the farmhouse.

"Six o'clock good for you?" he said.

"You're cooking?" she answered. "Of course!"

He tapped the car door. "Oh! And I owe you for the bait." She smiled without a word and drove away.

STEPHEN HAD ALWAYS COOKED FOR HIMSELF but not for guests except Paul O'Connor occasionally. A menu for his first true guests was intimidating and he thought of his friends in Atlanta. *Where is Madeline Reynolds when I need her?*

It would also be the first time since he'd come that conversation with others would break the silence of the farmhouse walls. He searched through his cabinet and refrigerator and the menu came together. It would have to be simple—his goal was to get acquainted with his new friends rather than have them judge his culinary skills.

He checked his table setting and reached for a tasting spoon to sample the sauce simmering on the stove. "Not bad," he said to himself, and added a touch more pepper.

The six o'clock hour arrived, and through the window, he could see Comfort walking up the gravel drive. A car was making its way behind him in the distance. When it reached him, the car stopped, and he saw Comfort climb in. The sun had lowered in the sky to provide a rosy welcome for his guests, and he added another log to the grate of the living room fireplace. The home was wrapping him with what he needed to give him the replenishment he knew he needed.

He stepped out on the porch and greeted them. "Welcome," he said, pointing to the sunset over their shoulders. "Just in time to see the sight of this amazing display of color."

"God's artistry," replied Elizabeth. They entered the house, and she handed a loaf of bread and a bottle of wine to him. "Something smells amazing," she said.

"Thank you for the bread and wine." Stephen placed them on the dining table next to his communion set.

Comfort looked around and saw the family candlesticks. "Mind if we use these?" he asked. "The family always uses them when they have their dinners here."

"Of course. That would be nice," said Stephen from the kitchen. He stirred the simmering sauce and checked the heat under the large pot of boiling water. "Can I offer you a glass of wine or something else?"

"Yes, please. I'll have a glass," said Elizabeth.

"Water. Just water for me," said Comfort. Elizabeth nodded approval of his choice and glanced toward the kitchen. "What's for dinner?"

"*Favorite*," said Stephen.

Comfort lit the candles. "*Your* favorite?"

Stephen chuckled. "A dear friend of mine and a wonderful cook and hostess taught me to make a special spaghetti sauce. It became known by her family as 'favorite' instead of spaghetti and I adopted the name too. Have a seat. It's almost ready."

Stephen placed the bread on the communion plate in the center of the table and set three glasses next to the earthenware pottery goblet.

"I hope you enjoyed your introduction to the farm today," said Elizabeth. "How do you know the Randalls?"

Stephen wiped his hands on a towel thrown over his shoulder and took a seat on the table bench across from his guests. "I don't. I am here on a sabbatical." Comfort tilted his head toward Elizabeth, questioning the word.

"Would that be an academic or ministerial sabbatical?" asked Elizabeth.

Stephen looked at both of his guests before answering. "A *ministerial* sabbatical. The Chapmans—or Randalls, that is—apparently have a connection with our Methodist conference in Georgia. The bishop arranged for me to have a time of replenishment here before moving on to my next assignment. Until recently, I served a church in the Atlanta area."

The two guests sat silent upon learning of Stephen's true identity and the reason for his stay at the farm. Stephen allowed for questions and hearing none, he served the plates stacked in front of him with the noodles and sauce on the table. He passed the plate of bread from the table center. "You honor me this evening," he said and raised his glass and pointed to the communion set on the table. "This was given to me by dear friends as a blessing for new friends on my journey."

Elizabeth raised her glass and Comfort joined her. "To new friends," she said.

The three took a sip of their drinks and Stephen asked, "May I offer a word of blessing for us?" Elizabeth and Comfort nodded and bowed their heads.

"Thank you Lord for this community of new friends. We ask you to send your transforming power to us as we seek to do your will in all things in response to your calling. Bless this food provided to nourish our strength for the journey that we will be truly grateful in the ways it will allow us to serve you. Amen."

They enjoyed their meal and Elizabeth smiled at Stephen. "Well... speaking of community," she said and glanced toward Comfort, "our small church certainly could not measure up to your big city one, but I hope you might consider visiting us during your stay."

Comfort chimed in. "I take the roses from the garden here for Miss Elizabeth to make our pulpit arrangement every week."

Elizabeth gestured toward him. "That's not all. Comfort is too humble. His woodworking is at the church as well. He has made many things for my preschool class. You should see the Noah's ark creation that we have."

"I'd like to," said Stephen.

The trio sat quietly eating until Stephen put down his fork. "You know, I've thought about our first conversation at The Mercantile...the one about the needs of the children here. Any updates on your concerns?"

Elizabeth leaned into the candlelight. "Well...should we call you Reverend?"

"Just Stephen, please."

"No ideas at this point. There is so much to consider. Funds. Staff. Volunteers. I suppose we could consider something at the church."

Stephen twirled his fork in the food on his plate, thinking. "I made a stop at Camp Greenwood this week. It sounds like they are having a similar problem."

Elizabeth glanced over at Comfort and back at Stephen. "Yes, it's a place near and dear to our hearts."

When dinner was done, Stephen served coffee, and they moved to the rockers on the porch. They talked about the differences between life in the small hamlet and the larger city but also discussed the similarity of needs. The evening came to a close when Elizabeth glanced at her watch and then at Comfort. "Busy day tomorrow. We should be going."

Stephen took their cups and stood watching as Elizabeth and Comfort walked to her car. "Oh, Comfort," he said. "Just so you know, I have a weekend guest arriving."

Elizabeth's interest in Stephen was peaked even more. "Well...they... are welcome to join us this Sunday also, of course."

Stephen smiled to himself. "Well, *he* has never been much for church. But who knows?"

Chapter 19

Starr sat on the apartment balcony soaking in the Friday afternoon sun. Her guitar lay over her. A pencil and empty notepad waited on a side table to record any notes that inspired her fingertips. "This shouldn't be so difficult," she whispered and strummed a chord on her Gibson.

A deadline was looming for her to report her progress to Perry Michaels. The feedback on her gigs at the Highland Avenue Tavern and other Atlanta clubs had been positive. This last task, though, would seal a long-term contract with his agency.

No musical phrases she played seemed to fit. *Perhaps it's my location,* she thought. *Or is there some other inspiration that would help?* Starr collected her cup of tea and moved inside. She looked at the words handwritten on notebook paper that Michaels had copied for her use. The subtitle to the words was "A Song for Jessie." She fumbled through her purse for Perry's business card and reached for the phone.

The receptionist answered. "Mr. Michaels is not in at the moment, Miss Chapman. Can I take a message?"

"Yes. I'm working on a musical score for him, and I was hoping he might give me some information on how I might reach a woman named Jessie. He will know who that is."

"I'll give him the message. He is on the road but checks in with me when he can."

"Thanks. A phone number. Anything that would allow me to contact her."

MATT LOOKED UP TO SEE HIS sister walking through the recruitment center doorway. She settled into the chair across from him and shrugged.

"Rough day?" he asked.

"In my line of work, there are always up and down times. This is a down one." Starr looked at her brother and winced, thinking how selfish she probably sounded compared to the down times and dangers he had experienced. "I'm sorry. I've never had such a creative block like the one I'm having with this song. I just needed to get out and clear my head."

Matt smiled. "No offense taken. I'm almost done here. It's the beginning of the weekend. Let me clear my desk and we can take off. We'll do something to help that head of yours!" He thought for a moment. "It's a nice day. Piedmont Park is not far and there's a park on the other side of town, they tell me. Out toward Buckhead. Chastain, I think is the name."

JESSIE HAD GIVEN MUCH OF HER time since the fall volunteering at Egleston Children's Hospital and at Piedmont Hospital. Even though her plan had always been to pursue a degree in Business Education at UGA, she realized she was drawn more and more to the causes that benefited children. Mr. Baker's encouragement to listen to the call of "about others" would not let her go. Mrs. Laney, her high school mentor and adviser, had commented that focusing on others might be something she will continue personally beyond her degree and professional career. Somehow, she felt her aspirations were changing, and she waited for some indication that would tell her which path to take.

Adding to her confusion was the call from Sandy. Blindsided, she couldn't get it out of her head. Rev. Hamilton had always been comforting to her since the loss of Carter. His questions to guide her thought process had been helpful, but as always, he couldn't provide her with all the answers.

Jack had taken seriously his promise to Carter to take care of Jessie when he'd left for Fort Benning. Watching Jessie grieve after Carter's death had been difficult—he hoped his support had been helpful to her in moving beyond the loss. But now, he was unsure. *Could Jessie ever see him as anything more than a friend?* The conversation with Coach had unsettled him even more. *Was his hope to spend the summer with Jessie in Atlanta just a dream?*

JESSIE STOOD BEFORE HER MIRROR. SHE shook her head and glanced down at the unfinished sketch of the old mill and reminisced about her time there with Jack. The outing had felt like a turning point for them but Sandy's suggestion that she should let him go had caused her to doubt her feelings.

The doorbell rang downstairs, and she heard her mother's voice. "Jack! It is so good to see you. How have you been?"

"I've been good...I hope it is all right to come by without calling in advance. Is Jessie home?"

"Come in. Of course, it's all right. Let me get her. She just got home from Egleston."

Jessie heard her mother call her and she took a deep breath. She bounced down the stairs into the living room. "Jack! I was just changing. The pediatric activities room was wild today! We decided to finger paint and it got a little out of hand!" Jessie smiled at him. "Remember when we went there to work on the class holiday project?"

Jack returned her smile. "Yep. Those children are great. It's good you have continued to volunteer there, Jess. I know Coach would like that." He paused. "Speaking of Coach, I just stopped by school to see him." Jessie was key in his decision-making about whether to work with the coach for the summer, but he decided not to broach the topic. "I took a chance you might be home. Tom and Claire—and Mike—are home too and hoped we might get together at the Caldwells." He would talk to her about it while they were at Tom's that night.

Jessie's first inclination was to jump at the idea, but Sandy's words kept swirling in her head. "Oh, I can't tonight, Jack. I have other plans."

Jack hesitated at her response. "Okay…well…maybe I could pick you up later and then we can meet up with the group?"

Madeline appeared from the kitchen with a plate of cookies. Jessie reached for the plate and turned to Jack. "Cookie?"

"No, thanks."

Jessie set down the plate. "Sandy called while she was home last weekend."

Jack was confused at the change of subject. "Yeah. She called me too. She asked me to come up to Knoxville for some big weekend coming up."

Jessie turned away from him. "You should go. I'm sure it would be amazing. I hear UT parties are a blast."

Jack turned her toward him and lifted her face so he could see her eyes. "I don't think so. Jess, what's going on?"

"Nothing." Jessie wiped at the coffee table with her hand. "Just a lot on my mind right now. You know, thinking about things...different things."

Jack waited for some other word to explain the sudden divide he felt between them but Jessie walked toward the fireplace mantle and again turned her back to him. Confused, he pulled his car keys from his pocket. "I guess I'd better be going then. Can we talk later?"

She managed a weak smile. "Sure, later," she said.

Jack left the room and Jessie heard the front door close. She parted the window blinds and watched as he walked, obviously deflated, to his car. Her mother stepped up beside her. "He really cares about you, Jess." Jessie hid the tears filling her eyes.

The phone in the hallway rang and Jessie quickly went into the hallway to answer it.

"Hello? Miss Reynolds?" asked the caller.

"Yes, this is she."

"I'm calling from the Michaels Agency. Mr. Michaels apologizes, but he's out of town and asked if I would call you. It's about your meeting with him and...Crow, is it? About the lyrics of a song you discussed?"

"Yes?"

"He signed a new musician and has asked her to work on a score for the song. She's asked if you would agree to meet with her. Maybe give her some insights to help with the composition."

Jessie was surprised. "I guess I could do that."

"Next week perhaps? Would Tuesday afternoon work for you? Here at the agency. Say four o'clock?"

"Yes. Tuesday. I'll be there."

Chapter 20

Paul O'Connor looked around his bedroom to make sure he'd packed everything. His gas tank full, he was eager to get on the road for his trip to visit Stephen in Cross Hill. An early Friday afternoon departure would give him more time to explore the opportunity Stephen had mentioned about the camp in Greenwood.

He surveyed the memorabilia of his life on the living room shelves. His spirit brightened with a new resolve, and he reached for his car keys. His Coleman cooler sat at the front door packed with food items to share with his long-time friend and his satchel, beside it, contained notes about what he wanted to accomplish.

The route out of town he'd chosen allowed him to reach Cross Hill with a minimum of traffic and the afternoon drive passed quickly. As he came into town, he passed the produce stand Stephen had described, the landmark just before the green mailbox where he was to turn. The sound of gravel beneath the tires announced his arrival. Stephen, beaming, opened the front door to the cottage. "Paul! You made it! Welcome!"

Stepping out of his car, Paul gripped Stephen's hand and looked around him in disbelief. "Amazing. There's even a rose garden," he observed. "Your directions were perfect," he stopped to look around again, "and I am in awe."

Stephen carried Paul's large duffel bag inside while Paul reached for his cooler and the food he'd brought to share. He walked through the front door and heard the crackling of a fire in the stone fireplace. "I just need to take this all in, Stephen. Now I know why it's named Comfort."

"Well," said Stephen, "that's another story, but this *is* a home away from home, for sure. No city life hustle and bustle. I have to admit the slow pace of the country has captured my soul. It took a while but I am now embracing it for all it's worth." He pointed down the hallway toward the bedrooms. "The Randalls have provided such a healing gift to folks like me. Let me show you the spare."

Stephen had prepared a roasted chicken for Paul's first evening meal. A freshly baked loaf from The Mercantile sat on the wooden board next to his cherished communion set. He brought out bowls with sides of seasoned greens and butter peas. Paul had never felt a reprieve of his daily tensions like he had when he'd passed through the farmhouse door. He grinned at Stephen. "Are those fishing poles for looks or for the guests here?"

"Most definitely for the guests," said Stephen. "We'll take them out for a test drive tomorrow. The Mercantile store manager gave me some new line and lures, and she dropped off some bait yesterday."

"She?"

"Yes, she..." said Stephen, ready to deflect any jesting. "And...she has invited us to her church on Sunday!"

Paul raised his hands in denial. "Whoa! That is *your* thing."

"Now, now. Don't get all touchy. I told her it wasn't your thing. Rest up, my friend. Tomorrow will be a full day. I want to show you the camp and something nearby. There's fishing and who knows what else?"

The two friends talked late into the evening. Stephen finally cleared the table and washed the dishes before returning to the den. "The fire is almost out. Sleep in or not. We're not on any particular schedule."

The guestroom bed with its colorful quilt and an extra blanket folded at the foot was a welcome site to the weary traveler. A wooden rocker was in the corner next to a rack with hooks. The walls had photos of days gone by at the farm. Underneath sat a pair of boots and a woven fishing basket. Paul stretched out onto the down mattress that called to his need for rest. He settled into its depth with only the sounds of a few geese flying across the evening skies.

JACK KNOCKED ON THE DOOR AND Tom and Claire greeted him arm in arm. "Where's Jessie?" they asked.

Jack reached for a drink on the kitchen table. "She had other plans," he answered.

"I should have called her and invited her myself," Claire said. "I was hoping we could talk more about the wedding tonight."

"Something's going on. I assumed too much. You know the night at the bonfire. New Year's at Cherokee. I just read more into it than I should have."

Tom looked at Claire and she shrugged her shoulders.

"Beats me," said Claire. "That's not like Jessie."

Jack joined the others in the den. Mike slapped him on his back and Terry stepped up beside him. "What's this I hear about you and Jessie?" he asked.

Jack took a sip of his drink. "She's still having a rough time. You know. I guess with you both being good friends of Carter's, you have a sense of what I'm talking about."

"School kind of covered up my accepting that he's really gone. You are closer to it now knowing how much Jessie depends on you," said Mike.

Jack shrugged the comment. "Not sure she depends on me. Where did you get that idea?"

The two friends followed Jack out to the patio. "Hey, man. I was at the New Year's party and so were a lot of our friends. We all saw it," said Mike. "You two couldn't have looked more into each other."

Jack remembered the dance and the moment before Tom's proposal interrupted them. He'd been about to tell Jessie how he felt about her, but that and their recent time together in Athens seemed all for naught.

Suddenly, he wanted to be anywhere but there. "I'm heading out. I've got some things to do. Tell Tom and Claire I'll see them next time." Jack headed to his car to go home but the next thing he knew he was driving toward Longwood Drive.

JESSIE PACED BACK AND FORTH IN her room. She'd felt an emptiness since Jack had driven away that afternoon. She opened her drawer and stared at the medallion on top of Carter's last letter to her. Carefully folded next to it was the purple shawl that Coach had placed around her shoulders at the funeral. She unfolded Carter's letter and read it again. *The medallion enclosed is for you to remember how to move forward and open your heart again to love. Sometimes finding love means having to let go.*

Jessie's heart skipped a beat. She ran downstairs and called to her mother. "Mom! Can I have the car keys? I won't be gone long."

Jessie drove over to Memorial Park and pulled to a stop at the curb. The park was wrapped up in so many of her memories. She thought of the unexplained moment of peace and clarity she'd had after receiving Sargent Randall's letter.

The sun had set and only a few spaced street lights hinted at the park's creek bank beyond. She stepped from the car and leaned against the door frame. "*What am I doing here?*" she said to herself. "*What am I looking for?*" And then she knew. Carter's letter had told her what she needed to hear and every thought circled back to the friend who had been there for her time and time again. She glanced at her watch and saw the hour. Jumping back into her car, she took off toward Northside Drive and Tom Caldwell's Arden Road home.

"I'm sorry, Jack," said Madeline when she answered his knock on the door. "Jessie took the car and left about an hour ago."

"I'm sorry to bother you, Mrs. Reynolds. I thought she might still be here."

"I wish she were. She was tearful when you left earlier. I'll tell her you stopped by."

"Thanks. The group over at the Caldwell's wanted her to know they wished she had come." Jack hung his head. "I head back to school in the morning. Would you tell her goodbye for me?"

"I will," said Madeline.

Jack had hung his hopes for the future on his time with Jessie at Christmas, New Year's and then her visit to Athens. He'd wanted one day to bring happiness back into her life, which would be happiness for him as well. But something had happened—he didn't know what—and Jessie was pulling away from him. Coach O'Connor's offer of a summer job as his assistant loomed in his mind. There was apparently no longer a reason for him to refuse.

As he drove up the hill on Longwood, he decided he should focus on his classes back in Athens and accept Jessie's apparent desires. But when he reached Howell Mill, instead of turning left toward his house, he waited for the car coming toward him to pass and turned right instead toward Memorial Park. Maybe she was there.

When he pulled up to the empty curb, he heard only the sound of a dog barking at a nearby house. His instincts about Jessie's whereabouts seemed to have proven him wrong. Disappointed, he turned the car around and headed back toward home. His decision was made—he would pack and go back to Athens tonight.

JACK'S MOTHER STOOD IN THE DOORWAY with a box of food from Mason's. "Son, are you sure you want to drive back to Athens tonight? Your dad should be home soon from closing up at the grill and I'm sure he'd like to say goodbye. Wouldn't it be better to drive back early in the morning?"

"I'll be okay," he answered. "It's not that late and I need to get on back and prepare for initiation at the fraternity. Exams are coming up too. I'll call later this week. Tell Dad I'll see him soon."

Jack's parents had always trusted his judgment but his mother had never seen this side of her son. She placed the food box in the back seat as Jack loaded his suitcase in the trunk. She reached out for a goodbye hug and held him longer. She hoped he would have been more open about the real reason for his unscheduled departure. She grasped his shoulders and looked squarely in his eyes.

"You know if you need anything..."

"Yes, Mom, I know," he said. "I know."

Jessie knocked on the door of the Caldwell home and burst through to find Tom and Claire standing with Mike and Terry. She stretched to look toward the den and kitchen. "Where's Jack?"

"He left a few minutes ago," said Mike.

"And he looked pretty down," said Terry.

"Do you know where he went?"

Mike shook his head. "No. he wasn't here long. Didn't say where he was going."

Terry stepped closer to her. "Jess. Jack is one of the best guys I know… and as far back as I can remember, he has always liked you."

Mike tugged on her arm. "Let's go outside," he said. She followed him to the corner of the patio. "You know after the whole thing with Fran our junior year—her thinking she was pregnant and all—I learned a lot from Carter about doing the right thing and appreciating life." He lowered his head and then glanced up at Jessie. "But I learned a lot from Jack, too. Both of them taught me about respect and being the kind of person that I wanted to be."

Jessie shook her head. "Mike, someone told me recently that I should let Jack go. That I was standing in his way."

"What are you are talking about? Girl, he has wanted to be more than friends with you since way before Carter came along."

"I've got to go find him, Mike!" exclaimed Jessie. She stopped and turned back to her friend. "And…thank you."

Jessie left the Caldwell's as quickly as she had arrived and headed toward Howell Mill and the Masons' house. Her heart fell when she saw that the Volkswagen wasn't there.

Chapter 21

Stephen sat on the farmhouse front porch sipping his morning coffee. The haze across the meadow was slowly lifting and he marveled once again at the peace he felt with every motion of his rocker. The sound of the door opening caused him to turn and see stretching arms of his good friend, draped in the patchwork quilt from his bed. "It can't be seven o'clock!" said Paul.

"Yep. When was the last time you slept in this late?" asked Stephen.

Paul scratched his head and stretched again. "Never. I mean, that bed...I slept like a baby!"

"Nice robe you got there," said Stephen. "You want me to light the fire this morning?"

"I somehow felt this urge to wrap up in it. Looks handmade."

"That would be my guess. Like so many things around here and most with a story," answered Stephen. "I'll have breakfast going soon. Come and sit. The sunrise is amazing."

"What's on the schedule today? When are we going to see that camp you told me about?"

"The camp is definitely first on the list. Then maybe a ride back through the property and some fishing. Could be our supper tonight!"

"Perfect! I'm curious, though, about this camp."

Stephen leaned forward. "Could be just the place that has your name on it."

JACK SAT ON THE PORCH OF the Pi Kappa Phi house. He had arrived late in evening the night before and grabbed an empty sofa to sleep rather than bother with the Payne Hall logistics. The Saturday morning traffic was picking up on Milledge Avenue and the girls from the Zeta house were coming and going, waving at the pledges gathered on the fraternity house porch.

Before initiation, a work day for all the pledges was required. Jack had completed his assignment of scrubbing down the kitchen counters and cleaning of the room named for the "back-room bandits." A pledge brother joined him and noticed the Zeta girls across the street. He handed him a cold drink. "Got a hot date tonight?"

Jack took a sip and shook his head. "Nope."

"My girl has plenty of sorority sisters. I can fix you up."

"Thanks. I'll let you know. What's going on tonight?"

"A band party over on River Road. The Kappa Sig house. It's open to everyone. Why don't you come?"

Jack gave him a "maybe" shrug and stood to head from the porch down the shotgun hallway. "Maybe I'll see you there."

He grabbed a donut from the Krispy Kreme box on the hall table and continued to the back parking lot. He checked on his Volkswagen, which the brothers allowed him to keep at the house because of freshman campus parking restrictions.

He took the final bite of his donut. He cleaned his windshield and climbed into the interior to wipe the dash and upholstery. *I've got to snap out of this. Maybe a band party would help."*

STEPHEN AND PAUL DROVE DOWN THE highway toward Greenwood, Paul looking from side to side at the open fields and lake inlets peeping through tree openings. A left turn came soon at the aged Camp Greenwood sign.

Paul leaned toward the dash and frowned. "Is this it?"

"Hold on," said Stephen, "and keep an open mind. I know it looks rough, but you need to look beyond for the potential."

When he saw Abbott Charles, Stephen stopped and introduced Paul to the camp leader. Abbott was pleased to see Stephen's return and, even more so, to see he had brought a friend. "Let me show you our camp, Mr. O'Connor," he said.

The return trip to Cross Hill was a quiet one. Stephen glanced over at Paul several times. He turned at the Comfort mailbox and made a left down toward the lake. The horses lifted their heads to watch the unfamiliar car make its way down the road past the lake and out toward the north side of the property.

Paul rolled down his window to take in the air as they passed the pecan trees. "The land is beautiful."

Stephen drove on past the cabin and stopped at a fenced cemetery. "Elizabeth Satterfield drove me up this road and told me some of the family history—although I'm sure there is so much more."

Paul could see headstones down a stone pathway. "Mind if we stop and walk down there?" asked Stephen.

"Suits me," said Paul.

The small cemetery was surrounded by wire attached to hand-hewn fence posts. Spring wild flowers sprouted along its perimeter. The late morning sun called the birds to raise their voices. Some of the headstones were flat and barely legible and others rose tall from the ground in separated square plots. The surnames of Jasper and Chapman were the most common among them with dates going back as far as the early 1800s.

Stephen, a lover of all things historical, pointed to several markers around the grounds. The two friends separated and walked the enclosed area to read the headstones. Stephen stopped and read the inscription on a weathered marker with fresh roses placed across its grassy knoll.

Matthew Lincoln Chapman, beloved son and hero
September 18, 1930 – August 30, 1940
John 15:13

He dwelt on its significance and, in silence, repeated the scripture to himself. "*Greater love has no one than this, that someone lay down his life for his friends.*" He had read the same verse at Carter Powell's funeral.

He glanced over at Paul, who had stopped at a special plaque with an engraved quote attributed to Abraham Lincoln. *The best way to predict your future is to create it.*

Paul looked at Stephen, who was now standing near the gate. "It's remarkable to see words and quotes meant for survivors," he said. "To come way out in the middle of nowhere and see such a thing." He paused. "Why did we come here, Stephen?"

"That's a good question, Paul. That's a good question." Just then, several cardinals joined them, each taking its place atop separate headstones.

"You didn't have to say it," said Paul. "You know. The visit to the camp and all. It would be overwhelming to think what you're thinking."

Stephen looked up from the Chapman marker and shook his head. "So, what am I thinking?"

"I know I told you I needed a change...something more. But rescuing a camp that needs a *lot* of work not to mention a *lot* of money to get it up and running?" Paul pointed at the Lincoln quote. "Did you know this quote was here?"

Stephen joined Paul and read the Lincoln inscription. He shook his head. "I had no idea. I am just as mystified as you are. My earlier tour of the farm with Elizabeth didn't take us this far." He looked over at the cardinals still perched on the tombstones. It would be too much to remind Paul of the legend of the cardinal, he thought. But it gave Stephen pause to think of the losses of Ann O'Connor and Carter Powell well before their time. And now, an unknown story and quote had emerged from the cemetery sanctuary.

"Maybe it's time to head back. We'll get some lunch and if you're up for fishing..."

"A good idea," answered Paul. "A wager that I catch the most!"

"You're on!"

Starr opened the sliding door to the apartment deck. "Beautiful morning, isn't it?"

Matt turned his head and sipped his Saturday morning coffee. He smiled and patted the chair next to him. "It is. I saved you a seat." He paused until she sat down. "It must have been a late set at the tavern for you last night."

"Yeah. There was a no-show on the final set, so I stepped in. There was extra pay and tips, so that never hurts my lowly bank account." She looked out through the trees and took a deep breath. "Wonder what Mom is doing today? I need to call her. And…I wonder what my brother is thinking. You look far away."

"Not so far. Just thinking. I'll probably be hearing something about my orders soon."

Starr sensed loneliness. It had dominated his spirit since she'd joined him in Atlanta. "It's good to be here with you." She thought for a moment and then turned to her brother again. "Hey! What are you doing next Tuesday?"

"Same ole, same ole. You know. Work. Come home. Go to bed. Back to work."

"I have a meeting at Perry's office Tuesday afternoon. It's near you. We could meet up there and go somewhere fun for dinner. Maybe try a new spot!"

"Sure, why not?" He stood up. "Hey, let's get dressed. I'm up for a jog over at Piedmont Park. You game?"

"I'm always game! After that, there's a grill over near Tech I want to try. Mason's, I think they call it. Maybe we can check it out for a late breakfast?"

Chapter 22

Lunch at the farmhouse consisted of barbeque and coleslaw from The General. Stephen made a stop there and at The Mercantile to pick up several easy options for meals with Paul.

While he ate, Paul made notes about their visit to the camp. He took a final bite of slaw and laid down his pencil. "I know for sure we can't do this by ourselves." He looked at Stephen, now standing at the kitchen sink washing the dishes. "I mentioned something to Jack Mason when I saw him Thursday afternoon. He stopped by to check on a summer job at my Northwest sports camp."

"So, you're saying we could bring in some help from our Atlanta base?"

"Sure, why not? What you got? There's got to be some support from the folks here."

Stephen looked out the kitchen window with its view of the pasture and lake. In the distance, he could see Elizabeth and Comfort with the horses.

"HERE IT COMES," SAID ELIZABETH as she pitched another bale of hay to Comfort from the back of the truck. "You think that will hold them for the weekend?"

Comfort laughed. "The pasture is proving a good backup. They never had it so good." He glanced around the landscape. "I can get you the Sunday roses while you're here, if you like. I have some beauties this week."

"You amaze me with your green thumb. Will you have a new animal for our Noah's Ark?"

"Of course. Been working on it this week—and its twin! I can't disappoint the children."

Elizabeth wiped her brow with the back of her sleeve and looked up toward the farmhouse. Her curiosity about the young reverend had continued since their initial meeting at The Mercantile. She brushed off her jeans and tried to straighten the hair hanging in her face. "I told Jeb I'd get right back to the store after this. If you have time, we could use your help to unload a shipment coming this afternoon. If you do, would you mind bringing the roses by when you come?"

Comfort followed her gaze toward the farmhouse. "Sure thing."

JEB STEPPED OUT THE MERCANTILE DOOR when Elizabeth drove up. "The shipment came in early and the delivery guys helped me unload. Been a pretty good day for business with our regulars," he said.

She brushed more of the hay from her jeans and went into the store.

Minutes later, Comfort pulled up and she returned to the front with Jeb. "I asked Comfort for help with the unloading," said Elizabeth. "I'm sorry, Comfort," she called. "The goods have already been unloaded. But we can still take the roses over to the church."

Comfort slapped his head. "Miss Elizabeth! I forgot the roses!"

Jeb wondered what was up. The caretaker had never been late with—much less forgotten—his Sunday rose delivery. "It's getting about closing time. I thought I might take some of the bread still on the shelf down to the row houses near the mill. You guys want to join me?"

"That's a good idea," said Elizabeth. "The children should be out playing, and I know their families could use it. We can't let their parents' pride get in the way of our helping them. We'll call it an Easter gift. Let's make some baskets and I can add some of my flowers from the Garden Shop. Some fruit would be nice too."

"Comfort, will you join us?" asked Jeb.

Comfort was quiet and his imagination was spinning. He had seen Stephen and his guest ride out toward the cemetery earlier in the day. "We still need those roses. Miss Elizabeth, would you mind heading back for them? I could help Mr. Jeb with the baskets. The families know me down at the mill and it might ease their worry about handouts."

Elizabeth looked quizzically at Comfort. "I guess I can do that. But be sure and invite the children to church tomorrow."

CLAIRE CLAYTON AND TOM CALDWELL'S NEW YEAR'S engagement had been no surprise, but their friends had been shocked when they'd set the wedding date in May. Claire had been accepted for a transfer to Vanderbilt where she'd join Tom and continue her college studies, but it wouldn't be easy to begin married life as college sophomores. However, their parents had agreed with their plans and the church had an open date in late May after this year's classes were completed.

Claire's call to Jessie on Saturday morning was a welcome reprieve from her worry about Jack. "You didn't forget we were going to finalize the bridesmaid dresses today, did you?"

"Of course not!" said Jessie. Holding the receiver under her ear, she stretched the extension cord and walked to the mirror to comb her hair and then opened her closet door to search for an appropriate outfit.

"We have appointments at Davison's and then Rich's bridal this afternoon," said Claire. "They have the shortest delivery times. Missy is home, so she's going too. I'm so excited. It's really going to happen! I'll pick you up in an hour."

Claire arrived early eager for the shopping trip with her friends. Jessie opened the car door and hopped in the backseat. "Missy can get in up front," she said. Claire beamed as she ran through the list for her wedding countdown. She turned around to Jessie before pulling down the street to Missy's house. "I'm counting on you to keep me focused!"

Claire sat in the dressing waiting area while her two future bridesmaids modeled dress after dress for her. "I'm thinking the blue one. No, maybe the green one." The girls stood waiting each time to accept her decision. "No, wait. Try on the pink one again."

Missy and Jessie went back to the dressing room once again. "Hey, Jess, are you all right?" said Missy. "You have been awfully quiet. I hope this isn't making you sad. You know, about Carter."

Jessie adjusted the sash on the pink dress and opened the curtain and stepped in front of the mirror. "Do you think I have done something wrong? You know, being with Jack?"

Missy peeked from behind her dressing room curtain. "Where did that come from? You and Jack have been friends forever."

"That's just it. There are some who say it might be wrong although Jack is more than a friend to me."

Missy pulled Jessie into her dressing room. "What could be wrong with that?"

"I was told I shouldn't hold onto Jack. That I should let him go, so others could have a chance with him."

"What in the world are you talking about? Who said that?"

"Sandy. She said she and others want to date him. She said I am holding him back."

A call from Claire interrupted them. "I'm waiting, you two! We have another appointment soon. Are you ready?"

Missy hugged Jessie. "This isn't high school anymore, Jess. It's not about what others think. Who cares what they want! What do *you* want?"

ELIZABETH HAD TIME TO SWING BY her house, swap out her truck for her car, and make a quick change before heading back to the farm. At the mailbox turn, she glanced in the mirror one more time to place a strand of hair behind her ear before pulling up to the house near the rose garden. A stranger sat on the porch. She stepped from her car and shielded her eyes from the afternoon sun. "You must be the reverend's friend," she called.

Paul stood as she approached. "Yes," he said.

"Elizabeth. Elizabeth Satterfield. He said you would be coming in yesterday."

Paul was speechless at the woman's natural beauty and searched for how to respond. "Uh...I'm Paul. Paul O'Connor."

Stephen stepped outside when he heard Elizabeth's voice. "Hey, you two." Stephen looked at Paul and back to Elizabeth. "Hey, Elizabeth. Did you come out to join us for some fishing?"

"No, Comfort is helping Jeb with some deliveries to the mill families this afternoon. Somehow, he forgot to bring the roses for our church arrangement tomorrow."

"I have a bucket you can use for the roses," said Stephen. "Maybe you'd like to take a break and join us for a spell. There's an extra pole here. Paul is a longtime friend from Atlanta. He's one of the best high school football coaches in Georgia."

Elizabeth turned her view toward the lake. Paul caught Stephen's attention and gave him a "What's up?" look for the fishing invitation, but Stephen ignored him. "I've got the bait you brought by Thursday. Not sure we'll be having a fish fry for our supper, but it looks like a great afternoon for some casting of our welcome poles!"

"That bait is all it will take," answered Elizabeth. "Jeb swears by it." She straightened the skirt she had changed into. "But I might be a bit overdressed." She looked over at Paul. "A teacher?" she asked.

Paul stood mute. Stephen gestured to him. "Yes, and an avid gardener. Paul, Elizabeth has that garden shop in town I told you about." He waited for Paul to respond, but when he didn't, Stephen nudged him. "He can help you with the roses while I gather the fishing gear."

Elizabeth reached for the bucket. "Just a small shop. Nothing fancy."

Paul took the bucket instead. "Here, let me."

Stephen gathered the fishing poles. "She is too humble. I heard folks from as far away as Charleston come to shop there."

Elizabeth smiled. "Well, it started years ago as a high school project. Then I was captured by it—and all that nature brings. Therapeutic, you know?" she said.

Her statement caught Paul's attention. "Yes, I know exactly," he said. "*Where flowers bloom, so does hope.* A special quote I like to believe."

Elizabeth gazed at him. "How beautiful. I must remember that."

Paul carried the bucket with water Stephen had added and stepped down off the porch to follow Elizabeth to the rose garden. When the two had chosen all the blooms for the Sunday service, she placed the bucket on the porch. "I suppose I could join you at the dock for a bit," she said.

The three made their way down to the lake and found their spots along the dock and grassy banks. "The mill families…" said Stephen. "Are these some of the ones you expressed your concerns for when I was in The Mercantile earlier?"

Elizabeth looked out over the lake and lowered her head. "It's heartbreaking. They're such deserving children, but hard times have kept them from thriving. My Laurens class has been blessed and I just want to see our Cross Hill children have the same opportunities."

Paul straightened his shoulders at Elizabeth's reference to her teaching background. "What kind of opportunities are you looking for?" asked Paul.

Stephen chimed in. "Paul, I'm sure, can relate to your concerns. Interestingly enough, I took him over to visit the camp in Greenwood this morning. He met Mr. Charles."

"It's quite an impressive piece of property there," said Paul.

"Yes, it is," said Elizabeth. "Those of us who grew up around here all spent time there. But it, too, has fallen on hard times." She was quiet for a moment.

Paul cast his line further into the waters and turned his reel to discover a small brim tugging against him.

"You have a bite!" said Elizabeth.

Paul reeled in the fish and released it. "What would it take?" he asked.

"Take?" asked Elizabeth.

"What would it take to revitalize the camp?" answered Paul. "You know. For the kids here in Cross Hill."

Elizabeth placed her pole on the ground. "People who care. People who love children and want to see them thrive…like I do…and some backing. I don't know how much, but it will take quite a bit."

Paul looked at Stephen. He knew his friend had invited him to join him there to find myself. To find something more in his life.

The sun lowered into the horizon. "It's getting late. I need to get back to town and take the roses to the church. Will you both be joining us for services tomorrow?"

Stephen looked at Paul, unsure of his response, and did his best not to make eye contact with him.

Paul didn't hesitate. "We'll be there."

Chapter 23

Jack took his time choosing a shirt. He questioned if his decision to go to the Kappa Sig band party was right for him. His roommate Davis returned from the shower and threw his wet towel on the floor. "Heading over to River Road?"

"Probably. I think I'll walk," answered Jack.

"Well. A bunch of girls from Villa Rica are up for the weekend. There's a keg party out at Callaway Gardens." Davis ran a quick comb through his hair. "Still time to change your mind."

"I'm meeting some of the brothers at the Kappa Sig house."

"Man. You're sure into that whole frat scene, aren't you?" said Davis. He shook his head. "Too many rules for me."

The clothes piled in the corner on Davis's side of the room were overflowing. He rummaged through his dresser and came up with a plaid shirt, one with the least wrinkles. "Suit yourself."

It was a clear night and Jack took the walkway behind the empty stadium next to the railroad tracks. He couldn't help thinking about how not long ago at the G-Day game, Jessie had been by his side in the stands.

Cars were passing and horns honking in anticipation of the party-filled Saturday evening. Jack stuck his hands in his pockets as he walked along the sidewalk and gave himself a pep talk. *This will be good. Get out there and have some fun.* He looked both ways and headed toward echoes of music coming from across the road.

The windows and doors were open at the fraternity house and cars were double parked in the fraternity lot and down River Road as far as Jack could see. The sounds from the house announced a large crowd and a party well underway. A travel bus was parked near the house with *The Tams* written on its side.

Jack passed several couples in the parking lot with arms wrapped around each other. Other brothers had come out for a smoke and get beverages being served from the trunk of one of the cars. One young man poured a cup of beer from a tap and handed it to him when he passed.

Jack took the cup and nodded. "Thanks."

A brother waved him toward the white columned front porch doorway. "The party's in the lodge room in back."

Jack made his way weaving through the students inside. He could see the shoulders of students swaying back and forth. There were shouts and drink cups overflowing without worry of beer spilling down the backs of those nearby. The *Tams* stood with separate microphones and moved with precision through their choreographed numbers. The well-known band was cheered in celebration when the band began their signature song, *Be Young, Be Foolish, Be Happy.* People next to him were singing along.

Jack felt a tap on his shoulder and heard a familiar voice. "I know you. It's been months!"

He turned and recognized the girl who had been Jessie's roommate. He conjured up a smile. "Hey, Leigh. Good to see you," he said.

MATT SAT AT THE HIGHLAND TAVERN table and watched as his sister stepped up on the stage. She was perfectly in her element—it was obvious to him that she was meant to sing and perform. Her enthusiasm for her music radiated from the moment she spoke into the microphone to announce her first song. "Good evening one and all!" she shouted when she grabbed the mic stand. "Welcome!" She smiled at her brother and turned to the standing-room-only crowd. "Where y'all from?"

The names of cities and states from around the country and other shouts joined in acknowledgment throughout the room. Matt looked around to observe the people. He felt out of touch with the joy shared by the audience.

Starr played her guitar and the backup band joined in with a medley of songs hailed by different states. Whistles and hands shot up when she began each new tune.

Matt overheard a conversation from a couple standing near him. "I heard she was good, but she's great! Glad we were able to get in to hear her tonight." Matt looked up and smiled with pride. They looked at him and repeated the compliment. "She's good, isn't she?"

"Yes, she's great!" he replied.

When Starr completed her set, she joined Matt at his table. The couple nearby was impressed. Matt gestured toward them. "Starr, meet my friends. I'm sorry…I missed your names…"

"I'm Hunter and this is Stacey." The couple beamed and shook Starr's hand. "You are amazing!"

"Well, thank you," said Starr. "I hope you'll stay for the second set."

"We wouldn't miss it," said Hunter. He reached into his jacket and handed her a card with a Nashville address. "I'm not in town long, but I'd like to hear more. Who is your agent?"

"Perry Michaels. Here in Atlanta," said Starr.

"I know of Perry. He's a good rep." Matt watched Hunter as he and Starr ended their conversation and the couple walked toward the bar for a refill.

Starr looked down at the card and gasped. "Hunter Anderson. This guy represents a major talent agency in Nashville!"

THE MUSIC TOOK ON A SLOWER pace and Jack heard the band begin the words of *Untie Me*. Jack suggested he and Leigh step outside.

"I haven't seen you since that day in our dorm. How's Jessie doing?" asked Leigh. "I haven't heard from her since the funeral."

Jack struggled to find the right answer. "She was here earlier for the G-Day game. It was a short weekend and she stayed at the sorority house. I'm sure she would have liked to have seen you."

Leigh wrinkled her brow in disappointment. "I told some of the girls on the floor about you and your support for Jessie. I guess you two are seeing each other now? I mean the G-Day weekend and all."

He wished he could have given her an immediate and positive response. He pretended the noise was too loud to carry on much of a conversation. "You here with someone?" he asked.

She pointed to some girlfriends, arm-in-arm with cups raised high. "I'm here with a group from the Zeta house. I pledged this fall."

Jack heard the band crank up another set inside. "Hey, let's go in and see the band. The music out here sounds great, but we don't want to miss their floor show."

Leigh placed her arm around his waist and leaned closer to him when they reached the crush of the crowd inside. A fraternity brother passed them and put another beer in Jack's hand. He had lost count. "Thanks. One more won't hurt."

Leigh waved to her girlfriends nearby who gave their nod of approval of the handsome guy at her side.

Chapter 24

Paul was up early Sunday morning before Stephen and made a pot of coffee. The front porch called him as it would have at home. He walked to the corner to see the fenced rose garden and thought of his own garden back in Atlanta.

The difference from his home was the clear view of the distant sunrise and the tranquility he had felt since his arrival. It had felt good to help Elizabeth cut the roses for the church service.

"When Morning Gilds the Skies," said Stephen from behind him. "It's a hymn that comes to me on my mornings out here on the porch."

"I see," answered Paul, after a moment. "You know me. I don't know many hymns."

Stephen nodded and looked again at the horizon. "But you *do* know the phrase *I will lift up mine eyes unto the hills.*"

"Yes," said Paul. "*From whence cometh my help*. Thank you for sharing that with me when I lost Ann." They stood facing the sun, now higher and brighter.

"This has been a place of repair for me. It has awakened my heart," said Stephen. Paul turned a questioning face to his friend.

"What? Did you really not believe I needed this time away?" asked Stephen.

"No, but I am ashamed at how much I took you for granted. I always thought you had it all together."

Stephen looked away. "This place has been such a gift. When I first arrived, it almost felt like a punishment. You know, to be removed from all that was familiar and all those I love."

Paul was silent. Words escaped him, but he had felt an indescribable awakening too.

Stephen continued. "But I now see its purpose and know there is more to my purpose for others."

"And was it your purpose to call out *my* purpose?" asked Paul.

Stephen smiled. "There are so many people out there looking for such answers. If I can be a conduit or a channel for the greater good, greater happiness and hope, then my work, my calling has fulfillment. "

They both stood listening to the morning sounds of the countryside. Then Stephen patted his friend on the shoulder. "Let's get some breakfast and then get ready. As I recall, you *did* tell Elizabeth you would be at church."

JESSIE HAD CONSIDERED STAYING HOME AND not going to church, but afterward she was glad she had. Her long-time church friends were away at school and the place that had been her haven for so many years seemed different. But the words of her pastor's morning sermon had been a message of hope and her spirits were lifted by the passage of scripture his sermon had been based on.

When she got home, she went to her room to change clothes. She would make the usual Sunday afternoon trip with her parents to Woodstock to see Granny Reynolds. Without thinking, she wandered to her bedroom window as she had so many times before, to look for Carter at the Sunday afternoon pickup football game in Memorial Park.

She thought of Jack and how disappointed she'd been when he hadn't been home the night before. Reverend Hamilton had counseled her to look for the stages of grief as she experienced them. *Could she be ready for the stage of acceptance?*

Madeline was making Sunday lunch when Jessie appeared in the kitchen. "You were gone quite a while last night," said her mother. "And you missed Jack coming by. He said to tell you goodbye since he was heading back to school."

"I missed him twice. I wanted to see him before he left."

Her mother handed her a stack of dishes to set the table. "Jessie, I know there is a lot going on inside you," she said. "You have much ahead of you, and I know losing Carter will affect you and all of us for years to come." She reached for her daughter and hugged her tight. "Just keep listening to your heart and trust that taking one day at a time will bring you a step closer to where you want to be, what you want to do, and who you want to do it with. Your father and I pray for that for you every single day."

After lunch, Jessie went upstairs to collect her jacket for the trip and glanced toward her desk in the corner. Jack's football jersey was draped over the back of her chair. She opened the desk drawer and retrieved the pen and stationery she kept there. During the trip to her grandmother's, she would collect her thoughts. The sleepless night, the morning sermon, Rev. Hamilton's counsel and her mother's words all helped her know what to write.

Dear Jack,

Several weeks ago, I received a letter that changed my life in so many ways. I began this letter to you then—to find the words for what I could not express that evening when we were together at the river. And now, I'm still trying to open my heart and write what I know has been growing there for so long.

You have been my rock for more times than I ever knew… long before I met Carter. Your smile, your welcome, your protectiveness, and your care for me never diminished over our years together. It only grew. I see your gift of the gloves to keep my hands warm when you are not here, and they keep you close.

Our time together at Barnett Shoals and in Athens was wonderful. You were so patient with me, and it was there I felt real joy coming back into my life. But I was accused recently of taking advantage of you—told that I should let you go and free you to move on. At times like this, I feel like I don't deserve you as a friend, much less something more.

I look back and see so much and wonder if I waited too late to tell you what was in my heart. Grief, I am told, can do that to you…shut out the ones who care the most and certainly, the ones you love the most.

You have been a home for my heart, Jack. You asked more than once if I was ready for this. I AM ready and I want you in my life…more than just as a friend. If you feel the same when you read this, I am here. If not, I understand and wish for you all the love you deserve.

With all my heart,

Jessie

Back at home, Jessie reread the letter. Her sketchbook sat next to her, and she removed the front page—the sketch of the Barnett Shoals mill—and placed it in the envelope with it. Sealing the envelope, she wrote Jack's dorm address on the front. No longer confused and embracing her future, she added a stamp and placed it in the family mailbox.

THE MORNING BELL WAS RINGING AS Paul and Stephen neared the church. They passed the Mercantile and Garden Shop and Stephen glanced over. Though closed because of the Sunday services, he knew it was Jeb's habit to open briefly afterward for people to stop in for a last-minute item for Sunday dinner. Paul stretched to see beyond the pergola gate to the garden shop.

Down the road, a group of families walked together from the mill end of town. As they approached the church, the children broke away and ran to the church steps to greet the two Sunday school teachers waiting there, yelling their names. "Miss Elizabeth! Mr. Comfort!"

Elizabeth wore a sleeveless blue dress. Her hair was neatly held in place with a gold clasp that stood out from her sun-streaked brown hair. Paul leaned forward in his seat to get a better view.

The parking area was filling, and the two friends found a spot near the azaleas along the perimeter of the property. "It looks like it's a good thing we left early," said Paul.

Yates Bryan parked across the way and watched each person as they arrived. The children danced around the patrol car and Yates motioned them onward toward Elizabeth while keeping an ever-present watchful eye. He raised his head when the vehicle pulled in on the opposite side from his view. It had never graced the church parking area, so he straightened in his seat to observe.

"Small towns—everyone knows everyone," quipped Stephen.

Paul opened his door and stepped out. "Except us!"

Stephen grinned. "We can go inside to the sanctuary while the children have their Sunday school, but it would be nice to stop by their room and pay our respects to Elizabeth and Comfort."

JACK HEARD DRAWERS OPENING AND CLOSING and raised his head. "What time is it?" His head was foggy, and he thought momentarily that it was Monday and he was late to class. He squinted at Davis, who grabbed his coat and wallet.

"It's nine o'clock, man. You musta had some night! You *never* sleep in."

Jack rubbed his head and reached for his bedside clock to confirm the time. He pulled his legs over the side of the bed and looked out the window at a sunny Sunday morning. He tried to remember how many beers he had the night before and what had happened.

"Yeah, some night," he said.

"I'm heading up to the lake with the guys for some fishing," said Davis checking his wallet.. "You got any money I can borrow? My dad's letter didn't come this week."

Jack pointed to his pants draped over the chair with his wallet in the back pocket. "On my desk chair."

Davis didn't hesitate. He grabbed Jack's pants and reached in the pocket. When he pulled out the wallet, a small napkin fell on the floor. Bending over, Davis retrieved the napkin and read some scribbling on it. "Who's Leigh?"

"She's Jessie's former roommate. Why?"

"Nice note here—with her number. I'm beginning to think I should have joined your party last night instead."

STEPHEN WAS PLEASED TO BE IN a home of his calling. The building differed from his Sandy Springs place of worship, but the welcome by the members within the halls of the community church renewed the sense of familiar warmth he had missed. He and Paul found the doorway to the children's room. Stephen nodded at Comfort, who stood near the table on which Noah's Ark and its animals were arranged.

Elizabeth motioned them into the room. "I'm glad you decided to come this morning." Paul stepped inside ahead of Stephen. He was reminded of his visits to the Egleston children's ward.

"Which animal did you bring for us today, Mr. Comfort?" asked one child. Her eyes searched the ark and saw two new pieces side by side. "It's the geese!" she squealed. The pair had been expertly carved from a piece of burl wood and polished to perfection.

"Now give them their place in line, little missy," said Comfort. "We will learn more about them today."

Elizabeth glanced back at Stephen and Paul and pointed to two adult-sized chairs near the windows. She called for the children's attention. "Class, we have two guests today. I want you to show them how special you are and quietly find your places on your floor mats."

The young teacher had convinced the church leadership that the children deserved the largest classroom on the short hallway behind the sanctuary, but the furnishings were sparse. A nursery next door was full. The older children, youth, and adults gathered in the sanctuary corners or, when weather permitted, outside for their time before worship.

"Mr. Comfort is going to begin our group time to tell you about what his geese will teach us," said Elizabeth.

"Now, little ones," Comfort began, "how many of you have seen our geese flying high up in the skies?"

Many children excitedly raised their hands. "They honk!"

With almost as much excitement on his face, he continued. "And why do you think they are honking?" The children looked at each other in wonder.

"They honk to encourage each other," he said.

"I saw some geese and they made a big V!" said one child.

"They were following their leader, weren't they?" asked Comfort. He surveyed the room to make sure he made eye contact with every child. "Sometimes the leader gets tired. So, another one will go to the front and take a turn as the leader while the other one falls back with the other geese to rest."

Comfort raised his arms to show his muscles. "It takes a lot of strength to be the leader. But they stay together. We can learn a lot from them."

"Like what?" asked another child.

"Well, you know, I've seen that when one goose gets too tired or maybe feels bad and comes down for a landing, another one comes down to be with him or her. Like a friend, don't you know. We do that for one another too. If one of you are having a bad day or maybe gets sick, you can check on them and encourage them when they can't be out playing…or honking!" The children all practiced their honking voices and Comfort laughed.

Elizabeth joined them and signaled to Stephen and Paul to honk as well. The room was filled with the joyous sounds. Then paper and crayons were spread out at a long table and the children were invited to draw their own pictures of geese.

Once the noise subsided, Elizabeth continued the lesson, the children listening while they drew their pictures. She opened the Bible next to her to Genesis and read more about Noah and his animals. "Let's remember to think about what Mr. Comfort has taught us today. Like geese, we want to always encourage each other. We want to allow each other to take turns in being a leader and to always be a good friend when someone might be having a bad day."

Stephen thought about when he'd first heard about the lessons from geese—in a seminary leadership class. Paul mentally noted the message he'd received—he would share it with his football team.

MATT SAT ON THE APARTMENT BALCONY and listened to the quiet sounds of the early morning. The smell of bacon drifted from the apartment beneath him. A few rays of sunshine broke through a cloud, and he squinted to see a flock of birds pass overhead.

Growing up, Matt had heard about how Sunday was supposed to be a day of rest. He thought of the family farm in Cross Hill—it was the one place where he could embrace a sense of rest and restoration. Today, however, he was unsettled and restless. The chaplain had encouraged him to take some down time but looming in his mind was Lt. Thacker's "special" mission. His part in the exercise would be beyond dangerous.

Starr stepped into the doorway and whispered for his attention. "You know, Matt, you've got to get a grip."

Matt made a face but continued his focus on the morning sky. "Where did that come from?"

"You never talk about it."

"What?"

"Vietnam. I can see it in your eyes. You're there."

"I'll be going back soon." Matt stood and stretched his arms. "Get a grip? Starr, you didn't see what I saw. What I know is still there."

The two siblings had shared many experiences over the years and often called each other out. The good and the bad. Matt saw the concern in his sister's eyes—he knew she was only trying to help. He sat back down and propped his elbows on his knees. "Easier said than done, Sis, but I'm working on it."

Starr changed the subject. "Why don't we try that Mason's restaurant on North Avenue I was telling you about? We didn't make it yet for one of their famous breakfasts."

JACK HAD NO RECOLLECTION OF THE final hours of the party or any of the time he'd spent with Leigh. He couldn't even remember how he'd gotten back to the dorm. He had sampled beers in high school and an occasional cup of a "purple passion" alcohol concoction created at outings at the Tiger Den by the river back home, but his experience with drinking had been minimal compared to what he'd encountered at the fraternity. He had become familiar, though, with paying the campus drycleaner to take care of his sports coats after drinks were spilled on him by intoxicated brothers. This had been a first for him.

His roommate Davis's path had been different—Jack had left the young man sleeping most mornings, knowing full well he was cutting his classes. This Sunday morning hangover and the note from Leigh was not something Davis would let his "big city" roommate soon forget.

Jack resolved to focus even more on his classes—he owed his parents for their sacrifices to help put him through school. They'd agreed to pay for matriculation and room and board and that he could use his savings from his many odd jobs over the years to pay for his fraternity dues and activities, books, and supplies. He shook off Davis's ribbing and retreated to the library each night after dinner at the fraternity. Plus, it was the best way for him to concentrate and avoid Davis's Villa Rica friends, who hung out nightly in their room.

Davis always checked the dorm mailbox in Payne Lobby for packages and mail. They were frequently blessed with packages from Jack's mother, filled with baked gifts. The box labeled Mason's had become a regular Friday arrival and Davis was never shy about helping himself to its contents.

More important, though, Davis looked for the letters—and cash—from his father. Though meant for school expenses, he usually spent it on his weekend entertainment but it was only Tuesday afternoon, and his wallet was already empty. He stopped in the lobby by the mailbox, anxiously looking for an envelope from his father. "Anything for 212 – Mason or Whitlock?" he asked the student on duty.

"There's a letter for Jack Mason," said the student.

"I'll take it to him. I'm in 212," replied Davis. He snatched the letter from the dorm assistant's hand before he could protest and hustled up the stairs. He'd entered their room when someone yelled that the hall monitor was about to do a room inspection. Davis looked around—Jack's bed was neatly made, and his desk organized.

There was only one thing to do—open his desk drawer and sweep everything on top into it. This included the letter he held in his hand. Throwing empty sacks and bottles from the floor into the trash, he raced to the chute in the hall lobby and laughed when he heard trash from floors above falling through the metal passageway. He'd made it.

Finally, he returned to the room for a final check. All the surfaces were bare and empty. "Take that!" he mumbled with a final check of the room and headed to meet his friends, almost running into Jack in the hallway.

"Inspection?" asked Jack, trying not to smile.

"Yep, but I took care of things. I'm off. Gonna meet up with the guys over at The Bulldog. See ya later."

Chapter 25

The benediction bell was ringing as Stephen and Paul exited the church service and the two said their goodbyes to Elizabeth, Comfort and other members who had so warmly greeted them. Stephen headed to his car and turned to see Paul stopped to watch the families leaving for their separate ways.

"Why don't we stop at The Mercantile to pick up lunch? You haven't had a chance to meet Jeb Satterfield," said Stephen.

"Elizabeth's brother?"

"Right. Nice guy and very much a leader in Cross Hill. The two of them would be key if we decide to move forward with helping the camp and the children this summer," responded Stephen.

"What do you mean *if?*" answered Paul.

Stephen stepped in the car and leaned up to the steering wheel to his friend and grinned. "Does that mean what I think it means?"

"I need to head back to Atlanta after lunch, but this weekend has been a game changer for me, Stephen."

As they drove back to the farmhouse, Paul listened to Stephen's ideas. He had not seen such enthusiasm in his friend in a long time. At lunch, Paul pulled out his notebook and jotted down thoughts for a summer of hope for the community.

When lunch was done, the coach packed his bags for the return trip to Atlanta. Stephen went out with him to his car.

"I think we have a lot to think about and a lot to consider," said Paul, "but where there's a will, there's a way."

Stephen rested his hand on his Paul's shoulder. "Lincoln said it well, my friend. Predicting a future versus creating one at its best is challenging and inspiring."

Paul nodded. "You'll be hearing from me soon. Keep the No Vacancy sign out for that spare bedroom!"

MATT WAS FACING YET ANOTHER BORING afternoon. Closing up at the recruitment office amounted to completing his daily report which would be added to the end of the week communication back to his base command at Fort Benning.

The door opened and he looked up to see his sister. Upon seeing his expression, she placed her hands on her hips. "This isn't happening again!" she said. "Come on. You're coming with me."

"Where to?"

"It's Tuesday and I have that appointment at my agent's office. Remember? Then we are going to dinner." Starr pointed at his desk. "There's more to Atlanta than *this*!"

"Okay. But I'll wait outside. The evening's nice."

Starr rolled her eyes at his lack of enthusiasm. She would try again.

"You know that soldier's song I've been trying to score? I am meeting the girl it was written for this afternoon. Perry arranged it for me." She paused. "And after that, you and I are going to take in this town!"

Matt knew there was no sense in denying her, so he managed a smile. "I'll need to change then. This uniform is not the dress for taking in the town."

"All right, then. That's what I like to hear! You head on and meet me outside at the agency."

JESSIE DRESSED FOR THE MEETING AT the Michaels Agency. She read over the words of "Hope" many times trying to imagine what Carter was thinking and feeling as he wrote them. She'd read them before—the sheet Perry had given her had been unfolded and folded many times. She had preserved it in a clear plastic sleeve for the meeting where it would stay until it could be framed for her bedroom wall.

The receptionist welcomed her. "Good afternoon, Miss Reynolds. Please take a seat in the conference room. Miss Chapman should be here very soon."

Jessie smiled and entered the room, taking a seat on one end of the table. She pulled the protective sleeve from her purse and placed it on the table in front of her. She heard the receptionist greet someone else and turned to look through the door.

The woman seemed familiar. Jessie thought for a moment. and remembered the young woman waiting outside the agency door the day she and Crow had learned about the song. When the woman came in, she carried a guitar case covered in stickers from places around the world. These included an American flag and a US Army emblem. "Hello Miss Reynolds," she said, extending her free hand. "I'm Starr. Starr Chapman. Thank you for agreeing to meet with me."

Starr took the chair closest to Jessie and pushed back to open the guitar case. "You might think this is an unusual request. I hope you understand, but I have this voice speaking to me about this song." Jessie felt the blood drain out of her face.

"Are you okay?" asked Starr.

Jessie nodded. "I'm fine." She cleared her head and focused on the young woman. "That's an impressive case. You've been to all those places?"

Starr smiled. "I guess you could say that. I grew up in a military family. Traveling is my inspiration."

Jessie watched as Starr tuned her guitar. "How did this all come about? I mean Perry giving you this song?"

"Good question," said Starr. "It's the craziest thing. I was singing in Wilmington, North Carolina a couple of summers ago—one of the places I spent growing up with my mom and brother. The member of a band playing at the same time gave me Perry's card and I stuck it in my pocket." She laughed, remembering. "They were nothing like their name—the Playboys."

Jessie looked like she had seen a ghost. "The Playboys?"

Starr's smile disappeared. "Yeah. Did you know about them?"

"Yes. That was Carter's band. They were on tour there." Jessie pointed to the protective sleeve. "He was the drummer. He wrote these words."

"Wait! I remember him! The crowd went crazy on his solos! You mean he's the one who wrote this song?"

Jessie nodded her head, remembering. "The band did a lot of Beatles and Beach Boys and everything in between."

The two young women sat silently, both trying to reconcile their thoughts. Finally, Starr spoke. "Would you mind telling me about Carter?"

Jessie swallowed hard and leaned back in her chair. "No, not at all." She thought about where to begin. "Carter lost his parents in a car accident when he was six and his grandfather raised him and his brother. They were very close although he told me once that he felt like an orphan." Feeling her eyes well up, she hesitated to regain her composure. "His grandfather had been in the Army and always told Carter and his brother, Bobby, stories about his service. Carter vowed to make his grandfather proud. That was the reason he joined the Army."

Starr nodded. "I understand the whole military thing. My dad, my brother. It can take its toll, though."

"Carter had a lot of love to give to his family, to his friends…to me."

"I could tell that when I first read the words you're holding. You two must have had something very special."

"After his grandfather died, Carter's brother and their family minister, and his football coach were there for him," she hesitated and looked away, "and us."

Starr reached to touch Jessie's hand. "Is there something else that would be helpful for me to know?"

Jessie looked down at the final lines of the song. "Roses," she answered. "Red ones. They were his first gift to me and his gift at important times for us." She looked away. "I don't know if I have been much help. You know, composing the music and all. I didn't know he had written this until my meeting with Mr. Michaels. But we talked a lot about hope in our conversations. Hope for our future together."

Starr looked at her watch. "I'd like to hear more about you and Carter, but it's getting late." Her face brightened. "Say! Do you have plans for dinner?"

Jessie was surprised by the invitation but felt drawn by an unknown sensation to accept it. "No. I don't have any plans this evening."

Starr put her guitar in its case. "Great! Oh, I almost forgot. I hope you don't mind. My brother will be joining us!"

Stephen was sitting on the farmhouse porch when he saw the patrol car coming up the gravel driveway. He stood when Yates Bryan exited his car. "Sheriff, what can I do for you?"

"Well now," Yates answered. "A little conversation might help. I guess I first owe you an apology."

"I'm not sure I understand." Stephen motioned to the rocker next to him and the sheriff removed his hat and sat down.

"Well, you see, my first inclination after all these years being in law enforcement is to be suspicious of strangers. Sometimes it doesn't make me the most popular person in town. I've known the Chapman and the Randall families—Christine and her kids—for a long time and I'm protective of them. Over the years there have been some rough times." He glanced down the road toward the cabin at the driveway entry. "And then there's Comfort and that story."

"Story?" asked Stephen.

"Since you're a minister and all, I figured Elizabeth—or someone—might have told you about him. Hasn't really been my story to tell, but over the years I've helped keep an eye out for Roy too."

"He seems to have a very close relationship with the family—and Abbott Charles over at the camp in Greenwood."

"That camp was home to him in his early years. He has dedicated his whole life to this family and this farm, the camp, this town and the people here."

"I haven't been able to spend much time with him," said Stephen. "I think when he learned I am a minister, it might have created some kind of barrier to our getting to know each other."

"Naw. He finally got his heart in the right place."

Yates pointed toward the western section of the property near the family cemetery. "It started back when he was a little boy living with his family back there. The Chapmans and the Jaspers go way back. Even as sharecroppers in those days, the Jaspers were family to the Chapmans."

The sheriff gazed toward the cemetery. "Christine's uncle saved little Roy." Stephen raised his eyebrows and the sheriff continued. "Roy had wandered away from the family cabin back there all the way down to the lake, yonder." Yates pointed again toward the horse pasture and lake nearby. "Matthew couldn't have been more than ten years old and heard little Roy hollering. He ran to his rescue and got him to the dock, but not before he drowned himself."

Stephen remembered seeing the small wooden cross near the dock. It was all coming together in his mind. "Is that cross at the lake for him?"

Yates nodded. "That's why it's there," he replied. "Their son's name was Matthew Lincoln Chapman and they called him Lincoln. The family never blamed Roy or his family for the tragedy of losing their son that way. The camp over in Greenwood tried to help him along the way and the Chapmans always made sure there was a place for him there in the camp programs. But as Roy grew older and came to deal more with the fate of the one who rescued him, he began to drink and drink a lot. He just couldn't handle how it impacted the Chapmans. I had to get involved several times during some of his drunken episodes."

"You still keep a check on him?"

Yates nodded. "It's a small town, Cross Hill. I grew up in these parts too and we all look out for each other. Christine came along later, and her family spent their summers here. We sort of grew up together and well, we became good friends at one point." Yates paused and shook his head.

Stephen attempted to fill the silence. "I can tell this is a special place with special people. I'm sure there were and still are some good times here."

"Christine had a hand in that. She was…*is*…very special." Yates leaned back in his chair. "It was when the little ones started coming along in the family that Roy changed. On their visits they followed him everywhere. Even created that nickname when they asked about the bottle of Southern Comfort he always had with him." Yates chuckled. "They were too young to know it wasn't really sweet tea!" He paused. "Roy would sit watch on the lake down there to be sure none of them ventured there unsupervised. It was a turning point and I know the good Lord played a role in all that too. He saw the light when he saw himself in the faces of the Chapman and Randall kids."

"That explains the marker in the cemetery for Matthew Lincoln. I'm guessing Comfort puts the roses on his grave."

Yates nodded. "The rose garden he tends here at the house provides the ones for Lincoln's grave and the flowers each week for the church. The woodworking and carving his father taught him came into play too. He makes things for the house here, The Mercantile, the church and the camp."

"Anything I can do to help?" asked Stephen.

"Maybe. Elizabeth continues to fret about the children this summer. What's going to happen to them. She said you were in the store and mentioned collecting donations for the children."

"You know us ministers. Stewardship is not far from our thoughts."

"Summer will be here before you know it and not much time or money to help the children around here. Never had any kids of my own and I'm guessing you don't either." Yates glanced over at Stephen to confirm.

"You're right. I've dedicated many babies, but none of my own. My friend, Paul, who was just here—it's the same for him. But his being a teacher and a coach has made a difference in the lives of many, many boys and girls."

"I would say you likely have too, Reverend," said Yates. He stood and put on his hat. "I'd best be going."

Once the sheriff was gone, Stephen took a drive back to the gates of the family cemetery. He reread the quote on the plaque he and Paul had discovered. *The best way to predict the future is to create it.* Stephen had not thought of the farm other than as a place of renewal. Now, thinking about it again, he remembered that Bishop Clemons had said it could be a turning point for his journey.

Chapter 26

Between classes, Jack made his way across campus toward Science Hill and up Lumpkin past Lyon's Pharmacy. Lyon's had the best service for sandwiches, and he had just enough time to order one of their famous toasted pimento cheese sandwiches before his next class. It wasn't a coincidence that Lyon's was next door to the Alpha Chi house. Even though he knew Jessie wasn't there, something inside him hoped to see her walk out the front door.

"Jack!" His name rang out from across the street.

He turned to see Leigh trotting across Lumpkin. "Hey there," he said.

"Wait!" she called and headed toward him. "I kept thinking I might hear from you. You have my number, right?"

He searched for a way to change the subject. "How's it going?"

She fluttered her eyes and ran her hand up his arm. "I had a great time with you at the Kappa Sig party."

Jack continued walking toward Lyon's. "Just grabbing a sandwich on my way to class. Good to see you, Leigh."

"Wait!" she said. "Our pledge dance is coming up soon. Out at Poss's Lakeview." She oozed with charm. "I would love for you to go with me."

Jack wasn't sure how to respond. He had not been on the receiving end of such an invitation since the Northwest High days and the Sadie Hawkins dance. So far, he had dodged the attempted setups for dates at the fraternity, but now he was face to face with Leigh and had no excuses. He shifted his books to his side. "Sure. Coat and tie, I guess?"

"Great! Yes on the coat and tie, but you know how that goes. They come off pretty quickly. It'll be fun." Leigh tossed her hair. "I'll leave more details for you at Payne." She turned and bounced off toward her dorm. Jack looked at his watch and continued to the pharmacy.

Lyon's was accustomed to filling quick orders and he asked for his sandwich and chips to go and was soon back outside. He checked the traffic and crossed the street toward Myers Hall and cut through the quad up Science Hill to the Biological Sciences building. The 250-plus other students in the large auditorium rumbled with conversation before the professor arrived. He thought about his acceptance to Leigh's invitation and took a bite from his sandwich. He made an unsuccessful attempt to shift his state of mind to a future without Jessie and jotted a reminder of the date with Leigh on the front of his spiral notebook.

"I DON'T KNOW WHAT IS TAKING him so long," said Starr. "He said he would meet me here in the lobby after my meeting."

Jessie shrugged her shoulders. "Maybe something came up."

"You don't know my brother. All he knows is work. And given what he does, he knows nothing but promptness." Starr hesitated. "I guess I should tell you that my brother is in the Army. I thought he might be helpful in what we are trying to do with your song."

"Starr?" Jessie heard a voice from behind them and turned to see a handsome young man approaching. Clean cut and neatly dressed.

"Jessie," said Starr, "this is my brother Matt. Matt, this is the one I told you about. You know, the song and all. We just finished our meeting, and she is going to join us for dinner."

Jessie extended her hand to him. "Jessie Reynolds."

Matt's mouth dropped open as he took her hand. "Matthew Randall."

They looked at each other in shock.

"What is it?" asked Starr, but neither looked at her.

"*Sergeant* Matthew Randall?" said Jessie. Matt could only nod. "You came to my house. Your letter...I don't know what to say."

Starr stepped back, obviously confused. "What? You know each other?"

Matthew nodded again, this time to his sister. "Jessie received one of the letters I told you and Mom about, the ones I sent to the loved ones of the men in my unit. Carter Powell was one of them."

Jessie stared at Starr in disbelief. "*He's* your brother? I thought your last name was Chapman."

"Chapman is my stage name," said Starr. "It's our mother's maiden name."

Jessie thought of the indescribable feeling in the park the day she'd received the letter and composed herself. "My mother said you mentioned an assignment here in Atlanta."

"I apologize for showing up at your home that way. It was insensitive of me."

Jessie stood speechless. She had kept her emotions in check while meeting with Starr earlier but she could not hold them back.

"Why don't we head somewhere for dinner?" said Starr. "Jessie, you're from Atlanta. Where would you suggest?"

Jessie shook her head. "I don't think I can." She looked at Matt, her eyes were blurred with tears. "I'm sorry." She turned and walked away.

"But Jessie—" said Starr.

Matt touched his sister's shoulder. "You need to let her go," he said.

It had been several days since Starr had delivered her score for *Hope* to Perry's office. "Come in Starr," said Perry. "So glad you could make it back for our appointment so quickly."

"Are you kidding? My heart jumped when your assistant called. Is everything okay? I mean, I hope everything is okay." Her unfiltered chatter was a giveaway of her nervousness. "I mean, it came together pretty quickly, but I hope you'll give me another chance. I can make some changes."

Perry couldn't help but smile. "Relax…Hope is a great word to focus on for our conversation," said Perry. The receptionist gave Perry a thumbs-up and closed the door. He turned back to Starr. "Miss Chapman, the score and recording you left for me is quite…amazing. I have already forwarded it to my contacts in Nashville and it is getting rave reviews."

Starr stared at him, unbelieving. "I don't know what to say. You sent it to Nashville?"

"I have already been contacted by Hunter Anderson at Nashville Talent and Recording. You met him some time ago when you were playing at the Tavern."

"Yes. He gave me his card, but I never dreamed of anything beyond that."

"NT&R and the Michaels Agency have a great opportunity for you."

"An opportunity?"

"They are prepared to offer a major recording deal with a very lucrative agreement for the rights to *Hope*. It hit the right desk and the right ears at the right time. I have never been presented with this kind of offer so early with any of my new clients."

Starr sat up in her chair. "I'm not sure I understand, Mr. Michaels. What does all this mean?"

"Well, first, all things considered, I think you should start calling me Perry. Second, I know we discussed the issue about the royalties and the rights for Miss Reynolds. What we're talking about here goes well beyond any kind of financial impact to her. This is going to put *you* front and center in the music world. Your name is going to be known to people beyond your wildest dreams."

"You wouldn't just be saying that? I mean, I have had dreams of my career taking off, but this sounds too good to be true."

"I don't think so," said Perry. "When you told me about your visit with Miss Reynolds and then your brother's background and how that inspired your composition, I just had this feeling that we were on the verge of something big. The whole country is hungry for hope—much less peace and recovery. They are looking for something to make sense of what is going on here, especially in Vietnam."

Matt had met with several potential new recruits and completed his reports for the day. He had gained a reputation among other recruiting officers as a top enlistment specialist because of his frank conversations about military life and its challenges. His military family background was one piece of his stature among his peers, but nothing could replace his "boots on the ground" wartime experiences. When talking to recruits, he was truthful and his genuineness shone through…always with the faces of the men he had lost in his mind along with the hearts of their loved ones.

The other recruiting staff were checking out for the day, talking about their plans for the evening. Matt was planning to go to hear Starr play at a venue in the newly opened Underground Atlanta. "You go ahead. I'll close up," he said.

He glanced at the brochure rack in front and was in the back stock room gathering more forms and supplies when he heard the front door open. A late inquiry for the day, he thought. He returned to the front office area to find Jessie standing there.

"Matt, I want to apologize," she said. "About the other day and leaving the way I did."

"No. No. You don't have to apologize. You were caught off guard. If I had known—"

Jessie held up her hand. "I thought about our meeting a lot. And about your letter," she said. "I realized that when I looked at you…in a way, I held you responsible for Carter's death and that's not right."

Lt. Thacker's words of caution jumped into Matt's mind. "I don't want to bring you any more pain, Jessie. And Starr had no way of knowing about our connection."

"I know. But you were with Carter in his final days. All I can think about is the touch you had with him at the end. I want to say thank you."

Jessie's words set off a wave of grief in Matt that he had not been able to reach. He continued to stand in respect for her, but she could see that he was in pain. "Maybe we could talk? You know, finish—or start—what Starr didn't know she was beginning for us?"

Matt regained his composure. "I was about to close up the center. Would you be willing to have that dinner we were going to have?"

"That would be nice."

"I have some civvies in the back. I'll do a quick change and we can be off."

When he returned, Jessie was taken aback by how the change of his clothing transformed his image. Out of his uniform, he was no longer a stand-in for Carter, but an impressive young man whose smile and good looks lit up the room.

"Zeta pledge dance, huh?" said Davis, laughing. "Don't think I'll be getting an invitation to one of those." Jack's roommate shuffled through the papers on his desk and looked for his seldom-opened political science textbook. "That Leigh girl must be really into you. She's called you a bunch of times."

Jack, who'd been reading his English assignment, sat up on his bed. "She called? What do you mean she called?"

"Jeez. Don't get so uptight. Those girls always call back. Besides you have all those fraternity connections anyway. What are you so worried about?"

Jack shook his head. He had kept a level head with his roommate to this point. "Davis. I need to let you know after initiation, I will probably be moving to the house. The fraternity has offered up several openings and I plan to move."

"Come on. It was just a few phone calls."

Jack took a deep breath to calm himself. *I wonder what else he's forgotten to tell me,* he thought.

"W<small>HY DON'T WE TAKE MY CAR?</small>" said Jessie. "I'm guessing your car is not meant for socializing."

"It's okay, but you know the town better than I do," said Matt.

Jessie smiled and nodded. "Lived here all my life. Atlanta has changed a lot, but it's the smaller spots that I think you'd like."

"Sounds perfect. I *am* a small spot kind of guy, for sure," he replied.

The afternoon breezes were gentle, and Matt opened his window for the ride up Ponce de Leon and down Peachtree. He looked at Jessie with her hair blowing and the smile on her face. The breeze felt refreshing just like the conversation the two shared as she drove.

Jessie pointed ahead. "There's Pershing Point. That's where my dad's office is. I've spent a lot of time there over the years. I loved going there and helping him with typing his reports. I guess you would say my dad is the one who influenced me to want to teach about business. That is, besides Mrs. Laney. She was the best teacher." Matt looked up several stories to the third-floor windows Jessie had indicated. "It was an easy bus ride there from one of my first real summer jobs downtown. Now, that's a whole another story. Remind me to fill you in on Atlanta politics sometime!" she said. "And look to the left here. That's the Rhodes Theater. You should have seen my friends and me after we saw *West Side Story* there!" She laughed, "We were crying like babies."

Jessie pulled into the left lane as she made the curve around Peachtree. Let's go to the Crossroads Restaurant and Lounge. Great seafood and sometimes great music too!"

"It's been a while since I've had a good seafood dinner. Let's do it!"

They were early enough in the evening to find a parking spot near the entrance. Matt pointed across the street at a building. "What's that over there?"

"WSB. Our TV station. It looks a little different from the days I went

there to be on the Woody Willow Show. It was for a friend's birthday."
She laughed. "I haven't thought about that in forever." She hummed,
then sang. "*Hail, hail, the gang's all here. It's time for Woody Willow. It's
time for Woody Willow.*"

Matt laughed. He tried to imagine what a childhood like Jessie's
would have been like.

They stepped into the restaurant doorway. A gentleman dressed in
a chef's coat was at the entry stand checking the table listing with the
hostess. "Welcome to Crossroads," he said. He brightened when he heard
Jessie say, "I'm starving!"

"You've come to the right place!" he answered and instructed the
hostess to show them to their best table. Red rosebuds in crystal vases
adorned each table and Jessie's mood shifted back to reality.

Matt saw the change in expression. "Everything okay?"

"Everything's fine. The flowers just bring back memories."

The hostess seated them and told them about the night's special. Soft
piano music drifted across the room. "So," said Jessie. "Tell me about
you."

"Not much to tell. Just a country boy at heart but my sister and I
were raised in places around the world. My perspective about life has had
a lot of influences."

"Like what?"

"Well, my dad was military through and through, but my mom
balanced that with the stability Starr and I needed growing up. His
service took our family to places I would never have seen otherwise.
Mom helped me appreciate the simple things. Like our Chapman family
farm in Cross Hill."

Jessie almost jumped across the table. "Cross Hill?" She sat back in
her chair, a look of wonderment on her face. "This can't be happening,"

"What do you mean?" answered Matt.

Jessie shook her head and smiled. "First, your being Carter's platoon leader and your letter to me. Then, my meeting Starr and discovering you are her brother. Now hearing about the farm!"

"What about the farm?" asked Matt.

"The minister at Carter's church who has helped me so much is on a sabbatical now…in Cross Hill! He told me he's staying at a farm owned by the Chapman family."

"You know," said Matt. "I think Mom said Bishop Clemons had arranged for a guest from Atlanta to stay there. He must be pretty special for the bishop to arrange it with my mom."

"His name is Stephen Hamilton. And yes, he is very special. The farm sounds wonderful. I wish I could see it."

Matt smiled. "Maybe you can."

Chapter 27

Elizabeth had sent out flyers to the members of the Cross Hill community about a meeting at the town church to discuss the situation with the local children. She stood at the front and greeted individuals as they entered, thanking them for coming. The turnout was so large that Sheriff Bryan was out front assisting people in finding parking spaces. Comfort and Abbott Charles sat at the front of the church. Stephen stood at the back with Jeb.

Once everyone was seated, Elizabeth took her place at the front. Comfort's ark was displayed on the altar table next to her. "Thank y'all for coming today," she opened. "This has been a concern on my heart for quite some time. The children of this community are facing a summer with few or no activities for their benefit. Sheriff Yates is here, too. He can tell you what that means for some of them and how trouble quite often finds them. The good news is that I've met someone who wants to help us—along with some of his friends."

Abbott Charles stood and turned to the group. "Most of you know me. Over the years, I have seen many of your children come through the gates of Camp Greenwood. We have fallen on some hard times, just like many of you. But we're hoping we can change that."

Jeb joined his sister at the front. "Never had any kids of my own... yet." A rumble of chuckles ran through the audience. "But my sis and I claim all your kids when it comes to wanting what's best for them." He pointed to the first row. "Comfort, too." Comfort shook his head and raised his hands from his seat.

"Now, you see," interjected Abbott, "it's hands like those we need for starters. We want to have a workday at the camp. A day to clean up and make some repairs. With enough volunteers we can make the camp nice again."

"Then what?" asked a man in the middle row.

Jeb pointed to the back of the church. "Elizabeth mentioned someone here who would like to help. I want to introduce you to Stephen Hamilton, *Reverend* Stephen Hamilton." Heads turned all at once and Stephen acknowledged them. "He's staying out at the Chapman place."

Stephen walked to the front of the church. The bishop's words had never been more clear to him than now about stretching himself to discover what was next for his life.

"I'm pleased to meet you all," he said, pausing. "I have a very good friend—a football coach who has a lot to offer young people. He came to visit me here recently and we went over to the camp and visited with Mr. Charles. I think with your help, some other contacts of mine, and Coach O'Connor and some of his helpers, we can provide an outstanding camp experience for your children this summer."

A woman on the second row raised her hand. "I could help with cooking meals."

"Just got my tractor back from repairs. I can work on the grounds," said the man behind her.

Comfort stood and turned around. "I'll need some helpers with the building repairs." Several men raised their hands to volunteer.

Elizabeth beamed with the show of enthusiasm. "I will work with Coach O'Connor on the best possible activities if we can all pitch in to make this happen. My horses are available for riding lessons. We'll have music and arts. They'll be swimming and games. We often talk about our children's future. But their future begins with their *now*. What do you say?"

"Absolutely," said a man seated near the windows. "But what about money? I mean, I can help but I don't have much to give."

"We're starting here," said Jeb. "The Mercantile and the Garden Shop will be taking up a collection as well as donating some from our profits. I'll make some inquiries in Greenwood and who knows what will come our way."

COACH STOOD STARING AT HIS DESK in the athletic office. He had hung up the phone from a call from Stephen Hamilton and the report from the Cross Hill community meeting. He was forced back to reality when his door opened. The art teacher John Baker stood in the doorway.

"You know art doesn't have the issues of physical contact like football," he said. "But perhaps there is a mental side to art that could be a correlation to your struggle."

Coach squinted at his friend. "What do you mean?"

"You've always been the epitome of strength and being in control. You're questioning that control. We all do. But when we give up some or all of that control, we often find ourselves."

Coach shook his head. "How did you come to be so insightful? I mean, the kids here often quote you. Jessie Reynolds talks about thinking of others all the time."

"We've been friends a long time, Paul. And we have struggled together and celebrated together. You lost Ann and I lost so many dear friends in the Orly air crash years ago. Ultimately, losses like that make you face your own timeline and your own means of making a difference in this short time we have on this earth. You and I are left with little family. No children—except for the ones here at Northwest. You spoke about needing a change after you met with Principal Kelley. And I know you took a trip up to see the reverend. Did you find what you are looking for?"

Paul's eyes watched the faces of students passing by his office window headed toward the gymnasium. The message he'd read at the Chapman cemetery was still speaking to him. "I think so. You ever heard this quote by Abraham Lincoln? The best way to predict your future is to create it?"

"No, but it's a great one," answered John. He smiled and put his hand on the coach's shoulder. "You've got a great heart, Paul, and a lot to give." He stepped into the hall and closed the door.

Paul pulled his chair up to the desk and reached for the notepad with the beginning of his notes about the summer camp. His pen moved quickly down the page. The list was lengthy and he already knew who he would ask to help with each activity.

Chapter 28

The Zeta house bustled with girls going up and down the halls preparing for the evening's pledge dance. The counters in the common bathrooms were full of brushes, makeup and cans of hair spray. Leigh leaned in to wipe the steam from the mirror and one of her sisters passed behind. "So who's your date tonight? I haven't seen you spend this much time on your other dates."

"Jack Mason. He's a Pi Kapp," she answered. "I'm hoping it will be the start of something more. He is a friend of my fall roommate, Jessie. I've known a lot of great guys from Savannah, but there is something about him."

"Is she the one whose boyfriend died in Vietnam?"

"Yes, and Jack was there for her when she heard the news."

"So...he's just a *friend* to her. Nothing more?"

"I hope so," said Leigh. "I'll know better tonight." She smiled in the mirror and added her lipstick. "I know he would pass the 'Mom test.'"

The sister's eyes narrowed. "Your mom is pretty picky."

"We had a good talk when we were dress shopping. She was a little put off about his family running a grill in Atlanta, but I managed to keep her on board with the idea. She seems to think that everyone I date should be destined for a career on Wall Street!"

"And does he? Meet the future husband test?"

"Most definitely. I just have to bring on my A game and make sure he has no thoughts of anyone else but me. I don't have to worry about the whole family business thing with my daddy's connections."

JACK CHECKED HIS CLOSET AND REMOVED the plastic bag that covered a starched shirt from the Milledge Street dry cleaners. He looked in his wallet and double-checked his cash—he still needed to pick up the corsage Leigh had told him would be required for the dance.

A fraternity brother arrived to pick him up and take him to his car at the house. "I had my car washed and cleaned for the dance, but I need to get some gas after I go to the florist," said Jack. "I will need a fill up for that trip out to Poss's Lakeview."

The brother rolled his eyes. "You might want to think again about leaving your keys so handy at the house. I think some of the guys think your car is fair game."

Jack shrugged his shoulders. "After initiation, I'm moving to the house. That should take care of that."

The drive up Lumpkin took them by the Alpha Chi house. Jack's mind drifted—he'd not heard a word from Jessie since his last trip home.

"They're great," said the brother.

"Who?"

"The A-Chi-O's."

They turned up Rutherford and passed the corner of the Zeta house.

Girls were coming and going from the back parking area. "They're a good one too. Who's your date?"

"Leigh Alston. She's from Savannah."

The brother raised his eyebrows. "You mean of the Savannah Alston family?"

"I guess so," said Jack. "Why?"

They pulled into the back lot of the Pi Kappa Phi house. "We're talking big time Savannah money, that's all. Way to go, man!"

JESSIE HAD SHARED WITH HER PARENTS about Starr and the fact that the sergeant who had written the condolence letter about Carter was her brother. She had offered at dinner to show Matt more of the Atlanta sights, including Chastain Park and the stables.

The next morning, Jessie arrived at the stables and pulled the family Pontiac into the space near Powers Ferry. Matt was waiting and stepped up to open her door.

"You drove the last time. Now it's my turn."

"Where are we going?" Jessie asked as they left the parking lot.

Matt smiled and made a turn toward Peachtree. "It's a surprise." They continued through Buckhead toward DeKalb County and finally onto Buford Highway. When they reached the gates of the Peachtree-DeKalb Airport, Matt stopped. "Welcome to the home of one of my favorite things," he said.

Starr had mentioned Matt's pilot's license, but it never became a topic of conversation. Jessie took a deep breath and looked across the runway ahead. "You don't mean—" said Jessie.

Matt saw the look in Jessie's eyes. "Do you trust me?" he asked.

"Well, yes. It's just that I've never done anything like this before."

"It's a beautiful Saturday morning. The sky is clear and there's no better time," he said. "I have a Cessna reserved. You said you would like to see the farm, didn't you?"

"The farm? You mean we are flying to the farm? In Cross Hill?"

"Well, not exactly *to* it. Just *over* it."

Matt drove up to the guard station and showed his credentials. The guard stepped back and gave him a salute of respect. Matt continued to a building near the runway and looked back at the guard. "He's a great guy. We've become good friends since I started coming out for some flight time."

The runway was quiet. No other air traffic was in sight. Matt opened Jessie's door and pointed her toward the single engine plane sitting on the tarmac.

"I'm thinking my parents might not agree with this idea," said Jessie.

"I would never want to compromise anything with your parents, but I have more flight hours than you can count. I want you to feel what I feel when I'm in the air."

She stepped out of the car to the runway parking area. Another man walked out and gave Matt papers on a clipboard. He flipped through the pages and then guided her toward the small aircraft sitting in front. Jessie was nervous. "Why do you like flying so much?"

"Peace. Amazing peace. And it can only be described by experiencing it, Jess. We both have searched for peace from what has happened in our lives. In many ways we are connected by that."

The small door on the passenger side of the cockpit had a simple handle that Jessie found to be too easy to open. "Will that come open when we're in the air?"

Matt checked the wings and other parts of the aircraft and removed the wheel chocks surrounding the tires. "No way. Here." He took her hand to help her climb a small step stool to the wing and into the passenger seat. He checked the other side of the plane and slid into the pilot's seat. His thorough check of each instrument gauge and control calmed her.

He reached across her. "Let's get your seat belt good and tight. Those earphones on the dash are for you—we can talk to each other through the headsets."

Jessie took another deep breath—she had always been the one in the family to try new things and was labeled as the risk taker but this was more than she was accustomed to. She adjusted her position—there was just enough room for her to stretch her legs. She straightened her skirt and reached to grip her seat. "Has anyone ever called you a pied piper?" she asked.

Matt laughed. "That's a first! Thanks for trusting me. Don't be nervous."

The radio tower rattled off numbers and Jessie listened to Matt's responses. He touched the instrument panel and flipped various switches and the propellers turned. Matt reached behind the seat and pulled out an Army blanket. "When we get up a bit higher, the temperature will drop. You'll need this."

What is it with these men and their blankets? Memories washed over her. A high school blanket to cover her at football games. One draped over her after a dance. Another on a ride home after a special night at the Crow's Nest. She remembered the warmth of a basement throw from a sofa to cover her in a private moment and a special handmade Christmas quilt. There was something about the men in her life and their blankets of warmth and protection.

Matt looked at her expression and frowned. "Are you okay?"

"Yes," she finally said. "I'm ready."

Abbott Charles reached the Camp Greenwood outer gates and saw they were already open. In front of the main office were multiple cars and trucks. Beyond the gravel drive toward the swimming lake, he saw three new cedar picnic tables. Closer to the lake were a row of new Adirondack chairs. Hearing chain saws in the distance, he followed the sound to a clearing near the row of camper cabins and found Comfort directing five men.

"Roy! What are y'all up to?" Abbott hollered.

Comfort turned to see the camp director coming his way and waved. "Over here. Come see." He met Abbott on the path. "We had the wood donated right after the town meeting." He pointed to the men trimming weeds and brush. "With their help, it didn't take us anytime to build the tables and chairs."

"I'm overwhelmed," said Abbott.

"Now, now, Mister Abbott. We couldn't wait for you to get here. Everyone wants to pitch in. I know Miss Elizabeth is working on some plans. Let's take a look at the cabins and the camp kitchen and see what needs to be done."

Abbott shook the hands of several men and joined them in a walk toward the kitchen and canteen. Inside, several women were scrubbing down all the surfaces and looking through the contents of the pantry. "We could use some new utensils and pots," said one woman. She counted the number of plates and cups in the cupboard above the counter.

Jeb Satterfield walked in with a clipboard and an inventory list. "This will help us know what we have and what we need. My salesman at The Mercantile will be coming by tomorrow and I want to give him our order." Abbott heard sounds from the piano in the mess hall next to the kitchen and moved to the door. Jeb smiled when he saw his reaction.

A woman with a broom heartily swept the floors. Others with mops were not far behind her. Elizabeth sat at the piano. She played a few chords and winced. "We will need to have this tuned for sure."

Abbott shook his head in amazement and smiled. "I have a coffee pot in the office. I'll start some." Jeb and Elizabeth both grinned at Comfort and watched as he and Abbott headed outside.

The two men heard the sounds of an engine and looked up to see a small plane fly over the campground. As it passed over the lake, the plane dipped one wing.

Comfort recognized the move. "Look!" he yelled. "It's Mr. Matt!" Others on the grounds joined them and waved their arms in recognition. Once the plane was out of sight, Abbott opened the door of the office to find Stephen sitting at a chair next to his desk. "I saved your seat, Abbott. Coffee is ready and we have work to do!"

Jessie had felt the thrill of the take off earlier that day, but when the small plane made its final approach to the runway back in Atlanta, she found a new fear—landing. Matt was in full command of the controls and spoke to the airport tower. "Roger PDK. Heading south for final approach."

"Runway 16/34 clear for landing," said the tower controller.

The plane made its descent and Jessie's stomach turned as the nose of the plane pointed down. Matt could see the stress on Jessie's face and he reached to touch her hand. She opened her eyes to see the runway pavement coming up to meet the plane's wheels.

When the plane came to a taxi speed and headed toward the gate area, Jessie released her grip on her seat. "Whew!"

"You were a pro!" said Matt. He surprised himself when he leaned over to kiss her cheek.

"We made it!" she said.

Matt helped her make her way down the step at the wing and to the ground. Her legs wobbled and she grasped his hand. A gate agent joined them on the tarmac, handing Matt a clipboard. He signed the log. "Nice weather up there today," he said to the agent.

Jessie walked ahead toward Matt's car and he caught up with her. "Those people we flew over…they were at Camp Greenwood. I heard from my mom they are trying to rebuild and make a go of it this summer for the Cross Hill kids."

Now calm, she nodded. "The camp…and the farm was beautiful. I could see the people waving and the horses at the farm."

"You know when I tipped the wing as we were going over? They knew by that it was me."

They walked in silence for a few moments and Matt grew serious. "That town, that farm, has been my sanctuary. We named the farm 'Comfort' for a lot of reasons. Those people helped raise me. I owe them everything."

"It was nice to see…at least from the sky."

He paused again. "The Army is my life, but it can leave you empty sometimes. It takes a while to get to the farm by car, so when I'm stateside and nearby and need a quick reminder of all that's good in this world, I rent a plane and fly over."

Jessie thought of the many ways and times her Longwood home had been her sanctuary. "What else?" she asked.

Matt looked puzzled at her question.

"What else completes you, calms you?"

"Honestly?" he said. "Spending time with you."

Matt's answer caught Jessie completely by surprise.

Chapter 29

Claire and Jessie sat in the living room of Claire's house and opened a folder of to-do details on her wedding list. "The club wants us to come by and confirm the menu for the dinner," said Claire. Jessie's mind wandered to her New Year's date with Jack at the Cherokee Club and she didn't respond.

"Are you with me, Jess?"

"What? Yes, of course." Jessie waved a hand in Claire's direction. "I'm sorry. Your mentioning the club just makes me sad. I can't help but think of Jack. We had such a good time at the New Year's dance there. I thought we were moving toward something more."

"Wait a minute! You mean after that crazy comment from Sandy, you didn't work that all out with him?"

Jessie took a deep breath. "He never knew about that call from Sandy. I didn't want to tell him about it and make things awkward."

Claire stared at her. "So that's why you sent him on his way that afternoon and didn't go to the party at Tom's? When you showed up later, looking for him, I thought surely you caught up with him and worked things out."

Jessie shook her head. "No. I missed seeing him. He went back to school early. I sent a letter to tell him how much I cared. But that was weeks ago. I haven't heard a word from him since."

Claire reached for her friend's hand. "Jessie, you and Jack have always been more than friends. Maybe you didn't see it, but the rest of us did."

"I don't know. Now there's this Army sergeant who's come into the picture…his sister is the one that has written the music to Carter's song."

"And?"

"A letter he sent to me about Carter gave me a sense of peace I hadn't felt before. He even came to see me, but I wasn't home. And then, I met with his sister, and all of a sudden, there he was."

"What are you talking about?"

"Let me start over. I haven't had a chance to tell you, but you know that song *Hope* that Carter wrote the words to?"

"Yeah…"

"This girl came to Atlanta to sign with Perry Michaels. He was the Playboys' agent and Crow gave her Perry's card when Carter and the band met her on their tour in North Carolina. Perry gave her the words to Carter's song and asked her to write some music for it. A few weeks ago, she asked to meet me and the next thing I know, her brother shows up." She paused. "He turned out to be Carter's sergeant…the one who wrote me the letter."

Claire's mouth dropped open. "That is unbelievable! I know it has you confused. But don't get this sergeant mixed up with Carter just because he knew him and don't give up on Jack."

"Yeah, I thought about that, but when I didn't hear back from Jack, I guess I thought it was a sign."

Claire pulled Jessie closer to her. "Jessie girl, there are a lot of signs in the world. Seeing and reading those signs correctly are completely different things."

"What do you mean?"

"Well, like the sign I thought I had when my parents divorced. Crazy me thought it was a sign telling me that I should never fall in love and risk getting hurt that way."

"I don't know. I wish Rev. Hamilton were here. He could always help me make sense of things."

"You told me he said he was always just a phone call away," said Claire. "Maybe you could call him now. You still want to talk to Jack, right? Give it at least one more try."

"I've been so confused."

"And rightly so. No one could have handled what you've been through any better."

"I've tried, Claire, but it's been hard for me to accept the reality that Carter is not coming back. And now, I think I have to accept that same reality with Jack. He didn't respond to my letter and I just have to accept that. Plus, I *have* enjoyed spending time with Matt. There's something about him. And yes, there is a risk with him being in the Army—he'll probably be sent back back to Vietnam. But Jack has moved on and I will need to try to move on too."

Starr Chapman picked up the phone on the night stand to call her mother and catch her up on the news.

"They called Perry and they want to promote this new song you scored for him? That sounds so exciting, Starr!" said Christine.

With the phone under her chin, Starr placed the last item in her bag and sat down on the bed. "Yes. It's like the break I've always dreamed of. Everyone kept saying it takes a long time for the right song or the right person hearing it at the right time! I'm still thinking I'm going to wake up and it will all be a dream!"

"What does Matt have to say about all this?"

"Mom, you know I pretty much have the best big brother there is," said Starr. "He encouraged me not to give up. He told me that my day would come." She paused. "I just wish life would take a good turn for him."

"You've paid your dues, Starr. And so has Matt. You've both worked hard and given up everything to go for your careers and your callings," said her mother. "Now, see it through and have no regrets…and just remember where you came from and what your family stands for. *That* is what will see you through!"

Starr zipped her bag and set it aside. "Mom, I had a dream last night. I keep having this vision of the farm and Cross Hill."

"It's your roots, Sweetie. It's a big part of what made you who you are."

"And my music. I owe Cross Hill so much."

"When you get back from Nashville, we'll plan a trip to the farm and have a big celebration!"

JACK PULLED UP AT THE ZETA house. He brushed off the passenger seat of his car and glanced around. He was proud of the time he'd taken to clean it for the evening. When satisfied that all looked well, he followed other young men from the parking lot to the front entrance.

"She'll be right down," said the Zeta housemother. "These girls sure are excited about the dance."

"Yes, ma'am," replied Jack.

He straightened his tie and looked around. He shifted the corsage box to his other hand and thought about when he'd bought one before. His excitement about this date held no comparison to that one.

"Jack! Hi, handsome." He turned to see Leigh approaching. She was dressed to perfection in a white strapless formal that contrasted with a deep glowing tan. The dress looked like a bride's to him—and he couldn't help but wonder if her choice had been intentional. She made a sweeping turn, in expectation of receiving a compliment on her appearance but none was forthcoming.

Jack showed her the corsage. "I hope this is what you wanted," he said, suddenly realizing there was nowhere for him to pin it.

The housemother, who'd watched the exchange, stepped in to assist. "Would you like some help with that? I think it was made to be a bracelet."

In exasperation, Leigh grabbed the box from the housemother's hand and plopped the bracelet corsage on her arm. She moved to the lobby mirror to check herself again.

Jack saw the housemother's reaction and joined Leigh at the mirror. "You look very nice."

Pleased with his expected compliment, Leigh twirled in the dress again. "It's a one of a kind. My mother helped me select it and wants a picture of us. The photographer will be at the dance."

Jack was glad now for another reason he had taken the extra time to make his Volkswagen sparkling clean, but he was already dreading the rest of the night. "Ready? I'm parked on Rutherford."

"We can go out the back door," said Leigh. They exited to the parking area and Leigh gave Jack a sheepish grin. She pointed to a Lincoln with its motor idling. "Daddy ordered it for us!"

STARR SECURED HER GUITAR IN THE backseat—it was like her child. Several times, she glanced back to be sure it was safe during her journey. The drive through the North Georgia mountains and the scenery change along the stretches of Tennessee highway brought a smile to her face. Her heart skipped a beat when she pulled into the registration area of the Nashville hotel reserved for her. She gazed up at its multi-story grandeur and its welcoming canopy.

A valet opened her door and handed her a ticket and the hotel porter reached for her luggage. "I'll get that one," she said, reaching for her guitar.

She followed the porter into the hotel. When they reached her room, he went in first to turn on the lights and smooth the curtains on a large window overlooking the downtown Cumberland River. A welcome bouquet of roses and champagne from the Nashville agency were waiting on a buffet.

"This is the Regency Suite," said the porter. "One of our best." He reached for her ice bucket on the wet bar. "I'll get you some ice."

Starr grabbed her purse while the porter was retrieving her ice. At most places she stayed, tipping wasn't required, and she wasn't sure what to do. "Here you go," she said when he returned, handing him a five-dollar bill. She placed her guitar on the bed and opened her wallet again to count her cash—five dollars was a big chunk of her budget.

She had just enough time to unpack and freshen up before heading to her appointment. The wet bar was well-stocked with crystal glasses and a soft drink assortment. She chose a soda before exiting to the lobby. The valet asked to retrieve her vehicle.

She glanced over and saw her car parked close by. "No bother. It's the

Chevy with the North Carolina tags over there," she said.

He reached for her keys from inside the valet stand. "Oh, no, ma'am. You wait right there." He carefully drove her car around the fountain in front of the hotel and, with a tip of his cap, he opened the driver side door for her. "My name is Sam. At your service."

"Just a minute," Starr said and reached in her purse for his tip.

He raised his hand to stop her. "No, ma'am," he said. "Anything you need during your stay, just ask for me." Something about him made her look back in her rear-view mirror. He was watching her leave.

Her route took her along First Avenue to Fifth where she saw the Ryman Auditorium. She had always dreamed of standing on stage there.

"RIGHT THIS WAY, MISS CHAPMAN," SAID the agency receptionist.

Starr took a seat at the conference table in a plush leather chair and swiveled around, looking at nine empty chairs on either side of the long mahogany table. *I wonder what other famous singers have sat here,* she thought.

In no time, the door opened and to her surprise, a familiar face appeared—Hunter Anderson himself. An entourage of assistants followed and took their seats next to him.

"Starr!" he said. "It's so good to see you again. It's been a while since we met at the Tavern. How was your trip?"

"The drive was very nice. I love the beautiful Tennessee countryside," she answered. "Oh, and thank you for the lovely suite at the hotel. I am not accustomed to accommodations like it." She felt the blood rise to her face.

Hunter smiled. "Well, get ready. This is just the beginning. That is, if we can work out some important details." He looked to his assistants at the table. "I want to get Perry Michaels on the phone. Of course, we know he represents you and will be involved with our offer."

"Offer?" asked Starr.

"A very impressive offer, I might say," answered Hunter.

Hours later, Starr walked out of the talent agency, stunned. She couldn't remember where her car was parked, so she found a bench opposite the agency entrance and took a seat to absorb the details of the meeting. *This isn't happening,* she thought.

She reached for her parking ticket only to see that one of Hunter's assistants had validated it. Even though Hunter had offered to bring in lunch during their meeting, she'd politely declined—her stomach had been queasy throughout the meeting. But on the way back to the hotel, she realized how hungry she was.

When she pulled up to the valet stand, Sam stepped up and opened her door. "How was your day, Miss Chapman?" This time she handed him her keys without his reaching for them.

"Amazing!" she answered. "Say, where is a good place for an early dinner? I'm starved and I want to celebrate!"

"Celebrate?" He pointed to a restaurant across the street. "Best soul food in town if that happens to be your liking."

"Perfect! Nothing better than soul food," Starr responded. She headed toward the large revolving entrance door and turned back to see Sam loosen his tie. With newfound confidence, she returned to where he stood. "Excuse me. Are you off for the evening?" She was surprised, even to herself, that she'd dared to do it.

The valet's infectious smile and affirmative nod was all the encouragement she needed. "Yes, ma'am," he said. "It's been a long day."

"Would you care to join me? I hope the drinks are good there too!"

"Their drinks are very good. And absolutely. I need to clock out and change out of my uniform. Can I meet you there? In half an hour?"

"Perfect," she said. "That's perfect."

The phone was ringing in her room when she opened her door. She couldn't think of who could be calling—she knew no one in Nashville aside from the people at the agency.

She was delighted to hear her mother's voice. "Hey, honey!" said Christine. "I was getting anxious to hear from you! Did you have your meeting?"

"Did I ever!" answered Starr. "I don't know where to begin."

"Well, from the sound of your voice, I am thinking it went very well."

"More than well. I'll have to work through some details with Perry, but I met with Hunter Anderson. You know, the agent Matt and I met when I was performing at the Tavern. They have offered me a large—and I mean *large*—sum of money for the rights to the song I wrote the music for. And…a performance contract that will start right away! The agency has sent Perry the offer and he is reviewing it. We'll go over it tomorrow, but based on his reaction, I am going out for a celebration dinner in a bit."

"How wonderful. Are you going with this Hunter?"

"Uh…no. I am having dinner with a guy who works here at the hotel."

"What do you know about him?"

"Absolutely nothing, Mom. But besides Hunter, he is the only person in Nashville I know. And, by the way," she laughed, "I invited *him*. We're just going across the street for dinner. I am ready to celebrate!"

"Keep me posted and enjoy your dinner."

Starr hung up the phone and rifled through the clothes in the closet. She pulled out a dress suitable for a celebration and danced around the room with her guitar. "Baby, we are on our way!"

STEPHEN'S CALL FROM PAUL WAS THE response he had hoped for. The coach was definitely returning to Cross Hill and his ideas for the children's summer camp were coming together! With Paul's experience and enthusiasm for children, Stephen knew there was more than hope for the outcome the Cross Hill community was anticipating. Spreading the news of Paul's trip back to Cross Hill was a great excuse for him to visit town.

Elizabeth was working behind the counter when Stephen opened the door. She looked up and smiled. "You look like you've just won first prize at the county fair."

"You could say that. Paul O'Connor has agreed to come and take charge of the camp for the summer. He knows that with your teaching experience—and his—you two can plan some great activities for the children."

Elizabeth looked upward and folded her hands as if to say a prayer of gratitude. "Will he be here soon?"

"Yes. I told him we are still working on the fundraising side, but to leave that to me and the two of you can work on all the other details."

Elizabeth pulled out a notebook from under the counter. "I've made some more notes. Horseback riding and swimming, music, art, woodworking, nature studies, and hiking for starters. Comfort and the farm will be resources and you know how the community is stepping up."

"I met a farmer not far from town when I arrived weeks ago. He had a produce stand down the road across from a little church."

"You must be referring to Spencer…Spencer Adams. He has a large farm down toward Greenwood."

Stephen nodded. "He mentioned his wife and her cooking. I didn't know for sure, but he seemed the type that might help with the camp."

"Sure. Jeb knows them well. We carry their produce here in the store."

"Paul will be coming again for one more visit before school's out. I hope we can confirm all our volunteers by then. Will you and Jeb speak with Mr. Adams?"

"Of course. Thank you, Stephen. You have been a godsend to us."

He paused and noted her comment. With his ministry, Stephen had never been particularly thoughtful about what his calling meant beyond serving the people around him. He was, however, discovering the beauty of the simplicity of life that Bishop Clemons had counseled him to embrace. He smiled at Elizabeth and reached for the door of The Mercantile to exit. Even the simple ring of the bell on the door spoke to him.

He looked across Main Street to see the town's cherished church. The sun came out from behind a cloud and shone on its white frame steeple with a golden painted cross.

Jeb pulled up to the store in his pickup from making his deliveries and saw Stephen standing on the porch. He followed his gaze across the street. "You know it's more than a church building, Reverend," he said. The people here *are* the church. They have the biggest hearts."

Stephen turned back to see Elizabeth scurrying around inside The Mercantile in her excitement. "Indeed, they do," he said.

The arrival of the Lincoln town car at Lakeview drew quite a crowd. Leigh was well-versed in making the most of her sorority sisters' envy, and Jack was happy to step to the back of the group who wanted to see inside. He made his way to the bar and back to Leigh with drinks in hand. Leigh delighted in being the center of attention and waved him over to her side. He stood waiting for a pause in their conversation.

"Oh, Jack, thank you," said Leigh. She took the drink and sipped it. "My friends were just telling me that tonight some of the sisters might be getting a lavalier or pin."

Jack had avoided the early slow dances being played and heard the band's female lead step up and begin "You Can't Hurry Love." Leigh was into the words and so was Jack. *Love doesn't come easy for sure*, he thought.

Leigh leaned in. "I love this song. Don't you?"

He cleared his throat. "Uh, it is a good one."

"That was a big hit for The Supremes," announced the singer. "And here's one more!" The singer had the perfect voice for *Come See About Me*. They were well into the dance and Leigh was pressing even closer to Jack when he felt a tap on his shoulder.

"Hey, man. What are *you* doing here?"

Leigh looked at the young man, obviously irritated. "I beg your pardon! We're in the middle of a dance."

Jack's face lit up. "Terry! They let you out of the athletic dorm after dark?" The two young men exchanged high fives. "Terry, this is Leigh Alston. Leigh, Terry Whitaker. We played football together in high school."

Her expression changed. "Ooh…a football player," she cooed.

"Terry took being the Northwest High quarterback to a whole other level. He plays for the Dawgs now."

Terry reached for Jack's arm and looked back at Leigh. "You don't mind if we take a moment, do you?" Leigh could only say no.

Terry pulled Jack toward the high-top bar and grabbed another beer. "I have to say I'm surprised to see you here." He looked back at Leigh. "What's with her attitude, man?"

"Why are you surprised?" Jack glanced back at Leigh. "Leigh was Jessie's roommate. She invited me."

"Well," said Terry, "after seeing you and Jess at the G-Day game, I assumed you two were together."

Jack frowned. "Things were different then."

"Different? How different could they be? After Jess came looking for you at Tom's party back home, I thought you two were on a roll."

"What are you talking about?"

"That night at Tom's when you were so down, she came after you left, looking for you. I just thought..."

Jack shook his head. "I never saw her that night. She turned me down when I asked her to the party...like *really* turned me down."

Terry looked seriously at his friend. "Jack. You have always been there for me. Even when the whole thing with Natalie and her parents happened at Northwest, you had my back." Terry put an arm around Jack's shoulder. "It's payback time. And I know Carter would say the same thing."

"Come on, Terry. I'm not so sure. Carter just asked me to look out for her while he was gone, not take his place."

"And he IS gone! There's no disloyalty to Carter here." Terry leaned in closer. "Don't you see that he chose you for a reason?"

Leigh appeared and circled her arm in Jack's. "Hey, you two," she said. "You can catch up later. My guy owes me another dance."

Jack's eyes met Terry's when he heard her reference to their relationship. Terry raised his beer to Jack as they turned toward the dance floor. "Payback, Jack," he said. "I'm just saying...payback."

Starr and Sam consumed their dinner in record time and the conversation between the new acquaintances flowed effortlessly. Starr's eyes sparkled as she came to know more about Sam. They looked around—the crowd that had come while they were there was diminishing. "Look at the time," exclaimed Starr. "We have been here for hours!" Even with her early morning drive and the long meeting at the agency, she was more energized than ever. "Thank you for celebrating with me."

"My pleasure," he replied. "You mentioned wanting to take in the Ryman Auditorium. My shift starts later tomorrow. Can I convince you to let me show you around in the morning?"

"I feel like I've imposed enough on your time."

Sam leaned toward her and grinned. "Impose all you want, ma'am."

Paul backtracked to his office and bedroom to make sure he had all the notes he had made about what he wanted to accomplish. Several times during the nights before, he had woken to add another item to the list he kept next to his bedside.

He picked up the picture of his late wife Ann. His memories of her were filled with her constant encouragement to follow his heart. He looked at the kindness and love in her eyes that had touched so many during her life. *Am I doing the right thing? Can I really make that much of a difference at this camp? Is this the something more I am searching for?* He stood for a moment as if to expect an answer from above and then carefully replaced Ann's picture on his desk. Anticipation washed over him again. For the moment, at least, it seemed the answer was yes.

Paul exited to the driveway and glanced around at his cherished garden. The blooms of his roses were now opening. He could only think that the blooms were speaking to him.

Paul took a final glance back toward the living room before grabbing the last of his things and closing the door behind him. *Let's do this!*

THE MORNING WAS QUIET AS THE sun peeked above the horizon. Stephen stood in the kitchen pouring his first cup of coffee and listing items he would need for Paul's visit. He looked out the kitchen window and saw Comfort in the garden cutting roses. One horse was tied at the gate, waiting for Comfort to return.

Stephen realized he had never even wondered about Comfort's daily routine with the roses. He only knew that he provided them weekly for the church's altar arrangement. He took a sip of coffee and watched Comfort mount his horse and head down the stretch of road. He watched until they disappeared down the road beyond the lake's edge.

He stepped onto the porch and glanced at the fishing pole leaning next to the front door. This might be a good time to visit the lake dock and cast my line, he thought. He grabbed a biscuit and collected his lures and bait, and then headed on foot down the road. The remaining horses in the pasture rallied to the fence line and followed him.

Stephen took a last bite of biscuit and held the remains out to the mare closest to him. "Next time, I will bring you a treat! Think I'll catch a big one this morning?" The horse raised its head and shook her mane. "I'll take that as a yes," he replied.

The lake waters had risen with recent rains and he knew his chances would be better than most for a morning catch. He stopped at the dock and pondered again the cross at the edge of the water. A small bench waited for him to sit and cast to get a sense of the water depth. He closed his eyes and took a deep breath. The fragrance of honeysuckle called him to embrace what was left of his sabbatical.

He heard a voice behind him. "Careful there."

"Comfort! I didn't hear you come up!"

"Reverend, you best not be nodding off on *that* bench." Stephen chuckled but then saw the serious look on Comfort's face. The look took

Stephen to a place he had experienced often before—his pastoral care sense kicked in without hesitation.

"Won't you join me?"

"Got some chores waiting for me," said Comfort.

"I could help you with those chores," said Stephen. "But I sure would appreciate a lesson or two on the better casting spots."

When he'd learned that Stephen was a minister, Comfort had thrown up a wall—protecting himself from thinking about the heartache, blame and grief that had dominated his life. Stephen knew just enough of Comfort's story to stay open to a time when the two might talk.

Comfort stepped across the dock and pulled the line in on Stephen's fishing pole. He ran his hand down the bamboo frame and pointed up the road from where he had come. "I made this one from some cane up there near the old cabin." He took another careful step toward the dock's edge and cast it toward an area of standing grass, then handed the pole back to Stephen. "You'll find a nibble over there."

"Thanks," said Stephen. "You know, I find this spot on the dock a place of peace. That cross there has something to do with it. I'm sure it has meaning for different ones of us, but for me it brings peace."

"I wouldn't know," said Comfort.

"I have a friend who has searched his whole life for peace," said Stephen. "In some ways he still is. Searching, that is."

Comfort shrugged his shoulders and cast the fishing line another time. Stephen waited for his response. When none came, he continued. "Life has its many ups and downs. And there are many things in life we cannot choose."

Comfort glanced toward him and looked back over the water. Stephen cast out his line. "I've had my own times of questioning. When someone loses a friend. When a doctor's diagnosis for someone shakes them to the core. In the midst of it all, there is birth and joy. Like two people finding love with each other."

Comfort shuffled his feet and took a seat on the bench next to Stephen. He looked down at his feet.

"In the past, I've had nightmares and demons in me. Lots of questions and a load of hurting."

"There's no judgment here, my friend."

Comfort looked up to a spot in the distance. "The Randalls and Chapmans have been good to me and I can never repay them for the pain I caused."

Stephen placed his arm on Comfort's shoulder. "My buddy Paul is coming back this evening. He has had a lot of heartache and we've had this same conversation. We all need to find the meaning still there for us even in the midst of our troubles."

Comfort turned to Stephen with a questioning look. "Your friend? He liked his visit to Camp Greenwood, didn't he?"

"Yes. And so much of what got his attention was the work you had done there with the talent you have. The children there have been the beneficiaries of that."

Tears welled up in Comfort's eyes.

"Yes, Comfort, you are good with the children. You make a difference. A difference some of them might never experience if it wasn't for you. If we all could bring purpose to our lives in such a meaningful way." Stephen leaned back on the bench. "You know, some say that children are our *future*. But to me, they are more our *now*. They are our opportunity to put our own pasts behind us."

Stephen looked out over the waters and back at the small cross. The conversation was one of simple theology but a beginning for the two to build on to move forward in peace and hope.

✿

STARR STOOD AT HER HOTEL WINDOW gazing at the sun rays on the Nashville skyline. The special coffee brew she sipped was energizing—which was good, in that she'd had a night of little sleep. She thought of the meeting with the agency and her time with Sam.

The phone in her room rang. Anticipating a call from the agency, she quickly picked up the receiver. "Hello? This is Starr Chapman."

"How's my baby girl?" said a male voice. "What's this news I am hearing from your mother about a big break? Your mother told me where you were and something about a contract? When were you going to tell me about all this?"

"I just have a lot going on, Dad," said Starr. "Besides, you haven't been so easy to get in touch with yourself." She paused. "My contract is pretty nailed down and I have a concert to introduce a new single soon. I'll be singing with some big names in the business. It's overwhelming. How are you? How's Puerto Rico?"

"Doing just fine. My Spanish is still hanging in there," her father said. "What's that brother of yours up to? Did I hear right that he's stateside in Atlanta on desk duty?"

"He deserves a break, Dad. When are you ever going to give him a break?"

"You sound just like your mother. He needs to be a man and get back to the trenches like the rest of us."

Starr had often been the mediator of the family discord instigated by her father and was irritated by his timing. "It's nice of you to call to check on *me,* Dad,*"* she said.

"You just make sure they are paying you well."

Starr heard a knock at her door. "Sure thing, Dad. Gotta go." She returned the phone to its cradle and opened the door to her suite.

Sam removed his Stetson. "Did I interrupt something?"

"Not a thing," she said, glaring at the phone. "Your timing is perfect."

"Then, let the tour begin." He reached for her bag and she grabbed her guitar and they took them through the lobby and placed them in the trunk of her car.

Sam pointed across the parking lot. "My car is over here." Starr saw an Austin Healey convertible at the curb. She stopped to admire it and then climbed into the passenger seat.

The morning tour went by too quickly for both, but Sam knew Starr had to be checked out by noon and had one more stop at the agency before she'd get on the road back to Atlanta. He pulled up in front of the hotel.

"I wish I could stay longer," she said.

"Any chance you could change your schedule?"

Starr had thought about it, but had decided it was impossible. "I wish I could. Really."

Sam walked with her into the lobby and waited while she checked out and then escorted her back to her car and opened the door for her. She rolled down her window and he leaned in. "Safe travels," he said. "Maybe someday…"

Starr interrupted him and handed him a note with Matt's address. "Thanks for everything. If you're ever in Atlanta, look me up."

Chapter 30

Jessie was stunned. Perry Michaels had asked for a meeting so he could update her on the progress with Carter's song and his estimates of future royalties had left her speechless. She went straight to her father's office after the meeting.

"Dad, what does all this mean? What do I need to do?"

Ladd sat back in his chair. "I have had little experience with how royalties work but I do know business. There could be taxes and other legal issues. My banker would know—or at least find out for us." The First Federal branch office was on the first floor of Ladd Reynold's office building. The manager was a long-time friend and had handled Ladd's business accounts. He picked up the phone while Jessie waited. "Let me call Parker and make an appointment."

Jessie walked to the window to look out over West Peachtree and listened as her father spoke to the banker. "What did he say?" she asked.

"He is going to make some inquiries on your behalf and he can see us in about an hour."

The First Federal officer welcomed Jessie and Ladd into his office. "Based on what your father told me, Jessie, and how this all came about, have you thought about establishing a foundation or a non-profit or trust of some sort?"

Jessie looked at her father. She was unsure of what any of what the banker had said meant. "I don't know what options are available."

The banker continued. "Given what I know of you and your family and more so of what we heard about Carter and those in the military, I think this is an unexpected opportunity for you to make a difference to others in a significant way." He handed Jessie a folder. "Look these over and give it some thought."

Jessie walked with her father to the parking garage to head home. On the way, she looked through the folder. In it was information about different possibilities and a list of foundations invested at First Federal. She *could* make a difference for others. She closed the folder, held it to her heart and smiled. "I think a foundation makes sense, Dad. Let's call it the HOPE Foundation."

Matt was at his desk when the phone rang. He picked it up to hear his father's voice. "So! I hear you're warming a desk chair these days."

Matt steeled himself. "Nice to hear from you too, Dad," he said.

"So that's how it's going to be? More disrespect for someone who really knows how to serve in the trenches?"

"Did you ever stop to acknowledge what *I* have done or where *I* have been? I've never been good enough for you."

"Is that how that Army of yours teaches respect? I'll have you know—"

"I already know, Dad," said Matt. "No one will ever compare to you…least of all me." The silence on the other end of line was not a void Matt wanted to fill, but he continued. "Look, Dad. We've had this conversation way too often. Mom keeps up with my whereabouts and I hope your *son* will make you proud someday."

Matt hung up the phone and looked up at a fellow recruiter sitting nearby. "Some things never change."

Starr called Matt to tell him she was home from Nashville and Matt told her of their dad's call. "I've gotten used to his comments," he said. "And I ignore them. I know I am good enough regardless of what he says."

"Of course you are!" said Starr. "I know what you mean. He called me in Nashville, too. More concerned about what my pay would be than being proud of me."

"I can't remember a time when I thought he was proud of me."

Starr was silent for a moment. "Mom and I very proud of you, Matt. Don't let him get to you."

"I won't. I might take the plane up again tomorrow and fly over Cross Hill. After one of his calls, it always helps me to see the farm and remember the better parts of our roots."

Matt's joking manner did not fool his sister. "I think a flight is a great idea," she said. "Do a Cross Hill full circle for me too. I could use one of Mom's home-cooked meals at the farm soon."

Matt voiced his farewell to his sister. He hadn't told her that his conversation with Lt. Thacker would affect the rest of his day more than the call from his father, who'd never accepted that love and family were priorities over the Army. Matt's thoughts turned to Jessie—this was the first time he had considered his personal life over his call to service.

Chapter 31

Stephen and Paul had taken seats near the front with Elizabeth for the Cross Hill Methodist Church services. When they were concluded with a hymn and prayer, Jeb Satterfield stepped to the podium to call the church into conference.

"Thank you to all for remaining for this important meeting. As you all know, we have been working hard in advance of this summer to provide our children with some programming and activities to benefit them. Thanks to so many of you who have given your time and energy at the camp." He looked around the sanctuary to acknowledge those nodding their heads. "By now, most of you have met Paul O'Connor." He motioned to where the coach was sitting next to Elizabeth. "He has brought forward a wonderful plan in coordination with Elizabeth that is exciting. Both of them are volunteering their time for the entire summer!" Yates Bryan, who sat in a middle row, led the congregation in clapping.

Elizabeth stood to hush the congregation. "Now, here is the missing piece to all this. We need funds...contributions...donations of every kind to make this happen. There are still maintenance issues that we cannot do by ourselves to get the camp ready. We will be adding qualified staff that we must have to assure the children are well cared for and supervised."

The people in the pews looked at each other with questions on their faces. The town's resources were meager. Stephen jumped up and went to the front. "May I say a word?"

"Of course, Reverend. You are a part of us now too. We appreciate your idea of the donation jar at The Mercantile early on that got all this started."

Stephen smiled and nodded and then turned to the congregation. "Neither Paul nor I have children, but we come from a place where there are more resources. We both will commit whatever we can to keep moving forward. Thank you for trusting us with the lives of your children. We'll make the calls to secure the money and you do what you do best."

The congregation was quiet. Elizabeth was touched by Stephen's words and the commitment of two men new to their community. She stepped up by his side. "These men aren't the only ones who don't have children of their own. There are a number of us here today." She called attention to herself and looked at Jeb and Comfort. "But there are children here and elsewhere we have *called* our own. There are children no longer with us who made a difference in our lives." Comfort wiped a tear from his face and Yates quietly placed his hand on his shoulder.

"We all are blessed with gifts. I say we affirm this meeting to create the beginning of a new day for our children this summer," she said. "We have shared our faith in this community and embraced our hopes for tomorrow. We can do this!"

Jeb stepped back to the podium. "All those in favor, say "aye." The response was loud and unanimous. He looked toward the minister. "Now, Stephen, would you provide our benediction?"

It was the first time since the start of his sabbatical that Stephen had been asked to officiate in a service. He raised his hands in asking the congregation to stand with him.

> *Lord, we know that we are all your children. In every age,*
> *you have called us to be faithful in everything we do as we seek to*
> *follow You. Grant us today a clear vision of your call to fulfill the*
> *opportunity ahead of us. We know with the peace of hope that*
> *leads our lives, we can and will bring joy in the mornings of the*
> *days ahead. As we go now, reveal to us your promise of goodness*
> *and grace for the journey. For it is in the Name of the One who*
> *has spoken to our hearts…that we go forth in this calling to be*
> *Your hands and Your feet. Amen.*

ON SUNDAY AFTERNOON, THE LOBBY PHONE rang at Payne Hall and when Jack reached his room, he found a message on his door. An unfamiliar number was there with the coach's name beneath it. He placed his books on his desk and looked around at the room. On Davis's side was a stack of boxes…and a suitcase. A few minutes later, his roommate came in.

"What's going on? What's with all the packing?" asked Jack.

Davis shrugged. "Too much fun, I guess. My parents aren't the kind to keep paying tuition for D's and F's."

"Back to Villa Rica?" asked Jack.

"I suppose for now. Probably look for a job and get my act together." Davis picked up a stack of textbooks. "I know you tried to warn me. Guess I should have put these to better use. Oh, well. I'm off to sell them back to the bookstore."

Jack would move himself to the fraternity house soon, but his time with Davis had been a learning experience all its own. He shook his head to himself and headed to the door to call the coach.

"This doesn't look like an Atlanta number, Coach. Where are you?"

"A little town in South Carolina called Cross Hill."

"Not sure I've heard of it."

"Probably not. I'm here with Stephen Hamilton."

"The reverend? Tell him I said hello."

"I am hoping you can tell him yourself," said Coach.

"I'm not sure I understand."

"You know that conversation we had about sports camp at Northwest and all? I was checking to see if you were still interested in working with me."

Jack took a deep breath. His plan of working in Atlanta for the summer to be near Jessie had fallen apart. He had no plans other than work at the family business. "I guess so, Coach. Let me think about it."

"I could really use your help. Just one thing. The sports camp will look a bit different this year. The camp won't be in Atlanta. It will be here in Cross Hill."

Chapter 32

Matt shuffled the papers on his desk and focused on a report for his commanding officer. His new orders from Ft. Benning were pending—he wondered when he would have to confirm his return to a new assignment.

Despite Starr's encouragement, he still couldn't get the conversation with his father out of his head. *Don't let him get to you*, he thought, but the devil on his shoulder kept saying, *You've got to prove yourself to him.*

He checked the time. He had asked Jessie to join him for lunch and with renewed thoughts of her, his spirits were revived. He picked up his keys and headed to the door.

He knew Jessie had had a meeting at the bank, so they'd arranged a meeting place in Piedmont Park close to the recruitment center. Matt pulled up behind her and she motioned for him to join her in her car. "Hey there," she said, a big smile on her face. "Isn't this a perfect place to meet?"

"It looks a little suspicious to those people over there," he laughed. An older couple on a bench frowned at the younger couple's rendezvous.

Jessie laughed too. "Let them keep guessing," she said. Spontaneously, she leaned over to kiss Matt on the cheek, instantly realizing that it was a move she had never intended. But when Matt pulled her close and returned her kiss on her lips, she melted in his arms. She never dreamed it would happen.

And he had never intended it to.

When Leigh's Monday afternoon classes were over, she saw Missy Davis at the Creswell lobby mailboxes and remembered that she was a close friend of Jessie's.

"Hey Missy! I haven't seen you in a while," she said. "Not since that day in our room after Jessie received the call about Carter."

"Hey. It's a big dorm," said Missy. She looked at the pledge pin Leigh was wearing. "Zeta. Congrats. I went with A-D-Pi. I'm moving to the house next semester."

Leigh smiled to herself—the conversation was going exactly in the direction she wanted. "We just had our pledge dance Saturday night. Say, you probably know my date too. Jack Mason."

Missy eyed her with some suspicion. "Jack? Of course! He's great."

"We're *very* serious. I can't wait for him to take me to Atlanta to meet his parents!"

"Wow. *That* serious." Missy could not believe Jack would fall for anyone so quickly. She sorted through her mail and listened to Leigh gush on.

"Yes, and I expect his lavalier any day now." Leigh tossed her hair in regal triumph. "Take care. I'll see you around."

As soon as she was gone, Missy hurried to the third-floor lobby and picked up the house phone near her room. "Hello, Mrs. Reynolds," she said when she heard Madeline's voice. "Is Jessie home?"

The older couple stood and walked away upon observing Jessie and Matt's lingering kiss. When they pulled apart, they both sat in her car and stared at each other. Jessie felt a sense of guilt—she still had feelings for Jack, but he hadn't responded to her letter. Matt too felt guilt. He looked out the window. His life and future was about to change dramatically and getting involved with Jessie would be unfair to her.

Jessie could see the look on his face. "What are you thinking?"

"I was about to ask you the same question," said Matt.

Jessie bit her lip. "I think I need to tell you something. Something about someone very important to me."

Matt leaned forward and took her hand. "I think I need to tell you something also. Something that I just learned this week. But you go first," said Matt.

"His name is Jack. We have known each other since grade school and I guess you would call us best friends. He was there for me in many ways before I even met Carter. I know friends like Jack just don't come along every day. When Carter enlisted, he asked Jack to take care of me while he was gone. Ultimately, he was there for me, especially when I got word of Carter's death. He has stood by my side through everything since then."

"Sounds like a good friend," said Matt.

"Yes. But you see, I guess I began to feel something more than just friendship as time went by. These whispers that I keep hearing."

"Whispers?" asked Matt.

"Whispers that began when I took a walk in the park that day I

216

received your letter. Whispers that come to me at times when I feel like Carter is giving his blessing to my being with Jack."

"Oh, I see."

"But what you don't see is that when I realized that Jack was something more to me than a friend and I wasn't able to tell him in person, I wrote him a letter."

Matt leaned back and attempted to hide his disappointment. "Well, that's a good thing."

"But he never answered my letter. He never called and I have not seen him in weeks. That was just at the time when we connected through Starr and I guess I was just fooling myself that I should move on." Jessie smiled at Matt and continued. "You, our times together have been wonderful and this kiss...well, I just thought I needed to tell you that if we were to continue on with where we might be heading."

Matt nodded. "Our meeting through Starr and Carter's song lyrics, our times together whispered to me too. There was hope there in more ways than one." He thought about his pending orders and that their kiss might have been a turning point for his life. "But I am accused of being a man of few words, Jessie. This is probably one of those times."

"Matt, you have helped me find a peace that I didn't have. The flight up to Cross Hill and regaining trust that I needed. It gave me a whole new perspective on life."

Matt's mood had shifted and Jessie tried to read the look on his face. She could only guess she had interpreted their kiss differently from him. She took a deep breath in acceptance of knowing her true feelings had brought an honesty to their relationship. "You said you had learned something that you needed to tell me too?"

He shook his head. "It's nothing."

Jessie searched his eyes. "You're sure?"

"Yeah, it's nothing." The words of his father came back to his mind. For one fleeting moment, he had envisioned something more for his life but knew what he had to do. He looked deep in her eyes. "Thank you for trusting me, Jessie. Just know that I want what's best for you. Don't ever regret following your heart. Jack is a lucky guy."

Jessie searched his eyes and began to question him again. "Matt—"

He interrupted her and quickly changed the subject. He knew where her true heart lay. This would not be the turning point he'd hoped for. "Say, where's this place for lunch you wanted me to see?"

Confused yet recognizing their conversation had taken a less serious turn, Jessie started the ignition. She headed the car toward North Avenue. "Have you been to The Varsity?"

PAUL HUNG UP THE PHONE AND turned to Stephen. "I think Jack's on board. We can start filling out our staff and volunteers and complete that budget you've been working on."

"The money will come," said Stephen. "I'll be making more calls to contacts back in Atlanta. In fact, I called Ladd Reynolds last week to tell him about the camp." He gestured toward his friend. "Your activities schedule sounds impressive."

Paul turned the page in his notebook. "Elizabeth is going to take the lead on the music, nature, art—and probably add the horseback-riding element. But she'll need a helper. Someone with experience. Comfort is down for woodworking, gardening and heading up the maintenance department. Yates Bryan said he would help him. I would like Jack to be on top of the sports activities with me. I spoke to Spencer Adams, and he is working with Jeb to be sure all our food sources come together."

"I spoke with Bishop Clemons earlier," said Stephen. "He thinks the Randall family might be willing to let us use the farm here as a base of operations. I just need to keep making more calls."

"What does the bishop have to say about your sabbatical?" asked Paul.

"He just said ministry comes in many forms," he answered. "The more we work on this, the more I find myself looking toward a future I never imagined."

Paul shook his head in appreciation. "I can relate. I am imagining a different future as well."

They heard a knock on the door. "Anybody home?" Elizabeth stepped inside. "Y'all are not going to believe this," she said, "but Abbott just got a call from a bank in Atlanta!"

Chapter 33

"Come in," said Perry to Starr. "The coffee is fresh. *And* we have some fresh news from the agency in Nashville!"

She stepped toward the counter. "I could use a cup. I'm still recovering from all the excitement. I saw a tour bus parked downstairs. It has my name on it!"

Perry grinned. "Here. Let me get that for you. You're going to need to get used to being served yourself. The design graphic on the bus turned out perfect. Starr could not be a more perfect name for you. You're on the road to stardom!"

"My own tour bus? What's going on?"

"Let me put it this way. Royalties are rolling in. Our contract attorney is making sure all is in order for what is due and yet to come for your song *Hope*…and, by the way, here is your first check!"

Starr gulped at the amount on the check and looked up at Perry in disbelief. She looked at the check again and then back at him. "This is more than I have made in years on the road."

"And its only the beginning, Starr," answered Perry.

"I trust you have Jessie Reynolds' interest at heart, too?"

"Oh, yes. She's benefiting. Checks have started flowing her way too." He glanced down at his master schedule for Starr. "I see an opening next week. Do you want me to book you here until you hit the road again?"

"No. I would really like to spend a little time with my brother. Maybe head up with him to our family farm in South Carolina."

"Wow," said Matt. "That's pretty amazing, but I always knew you had it in you."

Starr shook her head in wonderment. "Thanks, Matt, but it's not just me. I mean, think about it. I got Perry's card from a guy in a band playing at the same club. Meanwhile you are the platoon leader of Carter Powell's company. You come home and write a letter to Jessie about him and then Perry gives me the lyrics to a song he wrote and asks me to write music for it. You take a position here in Atlanta, I meet Jessie, and *then* find out that the guy who gave me Perry's card was in a band with Carter. Matt, I heard him *play* long before you knew him in your platoon."

"Yeah, it's all hard to believe." The whole time Starr had been talking he had seen the faces—of Carter and the men he lost in the trenches. The military was the only life he had ever known. His commitment to it had always overshadowed everything else. The call from their dad kept coming back into his head.

Starr drummed on her guitar case and drew his attention back to her. "I know I need to play this smart. Who knows how long this popularity will last? Perry sounds pretty positive about it all, but I still can't believe this is happening to me."

She looked at her brother and saw his expression. How she wished his life had taken such a same positive major turn. "I was hoping you might be free to take a trip up to the farm. I told Perry I would like some time before I head out on the road. You know, to be with you and maybe head up to Cross Hill." She paused. "I already called Comfort. He said there are some guests at the farm and wants us to meet them. Sounds like there's a story there of some sort."

Matt shrugged. "I'm scheduled to work at the recruitment center today but we could fly up for the day tomorrow if you like."

"That works. I'll call Comfort back. He said he would pick us up from the airport."

"Hey, Missy," said Jessie's mother into the phone. "Hang on. Jessie is pulling in the driveway right now. She'll be so happy that you've called."

When Jessie came through the door, Madeline held up the phone. "It's Missy for you."

Jessie smiled and raced to the phone. "Missy!" she exclaimed. "I just got home from lunch. How's everything there?"

"Oh, you know. Lots of classes, studying, tests and all. Something I'm sure you don't miss!"

Jessie laughed. Even though her afternoon with Matt had had its ups and downs, her spirits were lifted and encouraged by hearing her good friend's voice. "I am looking forward to seeing you at Claire's wedding."

"I'm looking forward to seeing you too." Missy paused for a second. "Jessie, I'm calling about something else. About Jack."

Jessie's heart jumped to her throat. "Jack? He's all right, isn't he? Nothing has happened to him, has it?"

"No. Nothing has happened to him, but…" Missy told her about running into Leigh and what she had said.

After the call, Jessie slowly walked upstairs to her room and sat motionless on her bed. Jack's jersey hung on the back of the chair at her desk. Her sketch pad lay open on her bedside table with an unfinished drawing she had been working on. She picked up her pencil to continue sketching. *Jack is okay*, she thought. *That's all that matters.*

Madeline Reynolds opened Jessie's bedroom door. "Is everything okay with Missy?"

"Yes, she's fine. She heard that Jack is seeing someone. She said she was told it was serious."

"By the look on your face, I'm guessing that is not such good news."

"I guess that's why he didn't answer my letter. It's Leigh Alston. My old roommate."

She stopped to wipe a tear from her cheek. "I think I'll take a trip out to Egleston in the morning. It's been a while since I've seen the children and they always make me feel better."

PAUL STAYED OVER A FEW EXTRA days to continue planning for the summer. He and Stephen sat at the farmhouse table finishing a quick lunch before driving to the camp to check on the latest work in progress. "Let's swing by the Mercantile and pick up some of their fresh bread to take to Abbott. Maybe see if Jeb and Elizabeth have any news," said Stephen.

"Let me grab my clipboard," answered Paul. "I need to pick up a few other things and finish staffing." He paused. "You know, I was thinking this morning about Jessie Reynolds. She would make a great addition to the camp with her background in so many things—music, art, and horseback riding. And she loves working with children."

"That's a good idea. You should give her a call when we return."

They heard a knock at the door and Stephen glanced out the window. Comfort's truck was in the driveway. He opened the door to see him and two other people.

"Preacher," said Comfort. "Sorry we didn't give you any notice. This is Miss Starr and Mr. Matt. They—and their mother—own this farm. I told them about you and what you are doing here for the town and children."

Matt reached out his hand. "Matt Randall," he said. "My sister Starr goes by Chapman, but that's her stage name."

Stephen stepped back inside and enthusiastically waved them all inside. "Come in, come in! I am so pleased to meet you. This farm, your family's kindness and this community has been a real gift to me...to us, actually." He glanced over to Paul who stood, his keys in hand.

Starr smiled. "Comfort's been telling us about what you're doing for the children with the camp."

"They flew up this morning from Atlanta," said Comfort. "I just picked them up at the county airport."

"Atlanta? *Our* stomping grounds?" exclaimed Paul.

"Sounds like we have been trading places in recent weeks," said Starr.

Matt looked at Starr. "I am trying to convince my sister to take a break in her schedule and smell the roses."

"Good timing," said Comfort. "The rose garden is in full bloom!"

"Now, now. I *am* on an amazing high," said Starr. "Flying over the town, the farm...coming here gave me a much-needed reality check."

"In what way?" asked Matt. She shrugged her shoulders and walked to the cabin fireplace. She touched the framed military medals. "Above all, I want to be a part of something much bigger than myself. Part of the hope we all want in our lives for what is important."

"Hope," repeated Stephen softly. "That word keeps cropping up over and over again these days."

Matt put his arm around his sister's shoulder. "You're looking at someone who has put that word out to thousands of people," said Matt. "Starr is a talented singer and song writer. She just released a new single called *Hope*. And it's doing well—very well."

"I'd like to hear more," said Stephen, inviting everyone to sit down. Comfort stepped to the kitchen and reached for two earthenware coffee mugs.

"Well," said Starr. "I went to Atlanta recently to meet with a new agent. Matt is in the Army and there on leave for a temporary assignment, so we have been able to spend some long overdue time together. One thing led to another and the agent—his name is Perry Michaels—gave me the words to a song and ask me to write the musical score. We later discovered it was written by one of the men Matt lost in his platoon in Vietnam. I did write the music and then recorded it. Now I've been picked up by a Nashville group."

Paul glanced over at Stephen. "Perry Michaels? We've had dealings with him. He was the guy who hired Carla Peterson—you know, the girl who caused so much trouble for—"

Stephen stopped his friend. "Let's let this young lady continue her story."

Starr smiled. "What we didn't know until later was that the soldier was from Atlanta and that Matt had written a letter to his brother and his girlfriend."

"Yes," said Matt. "I wrote to all the families of the men in my platoon we lost. Carter was well respected by all the guys."

Paul stared at Matt. A shudder ran down his spine. "Carter? Not Carter Powell?"

Matt hesitated and straightened his position. "Yes, he was one of my men. You knew him?"

For a moment, Paul could not speak, so Stephen jumped in. "We both knew him very well," said Stephen. "Carter was a much-loved member of my church. I presided at his funeral." He gestured toward his friend. "Paul was his high school football coach, but he was more so like a father. Carter's life—from start to finish—was a testament to hope."

Paul collected himself. "We just spoke this morning about his girlfriend Jessie. I was planning to call her this afternoon. I want her to work with us here this summer—at the camp."

Matt and Starr looked at each other in disbelief. "Jessie?" he said. "Jessie Reynolds?"

FINALS OVER, JACK GATHERED THE LAST of his belongings. He looked around the room and smiled—when he returned in the fall, he would move into the Pi Kapp house.

The dorm counselor knocked on the door frame. "I'm making my rounds doing walk-throughs. Getting things squared away?"

"Just about," answered Jack. "Davis is already gone, and he left a mess. I'm cleaning out his desk. I'll have it done soon."

The counselor nodded his approval and continued down the hall. Jack pulled up a chair and a trashcan and opened Davis's desk drawer. He grabbed a stack of paper stuffed in the drawer and was about to toss the whole batch in the garbage when he saw his name and address on an envelope. The postmark was dated weeks before.

He stood and tore into the envelope and a folded sketch of the shoals fell out. He raced through the letter remembering their time together there. His heart stopped when he came to the end.

"You have been a home to my heart, Jack. You asked more than once if I was ready for this, and the answer is yes. I am ready and I want you in my life as more than a friend. If you feel the same when you read this, I am here. If not, I understand and wish for you the love you deserve."

With all my heart,

Jessie

When he reached the end of the hall, the house phones on his floor were all occupied. He took the steps downstairs in a couple of leaps, digging in his pockets for coins to deposit in the payphone. He grabbed the receiver and dialed.

Madeline answered. "Mrs. Reynolds. Is Jessie there? I really need to talk to her," he said.

"I'm sorry, Jack, she's with her dad."

"Will you tell her I need to talk to her, please? I'm coming home. I'll be there as soon as I can."

"Are you okay?"

"No ma'am, but I will be when I can see her."

"I'll tell her. But I think she has plans this evening…just so you know."

"I'll get there as soon as I can."

Several friends from the dorm passed Jack in the stairwell. He loaded his car as quickly as possible. He shut the car door and made his way back toward the dorm entrance for one last load. He needed to check out with the dorm counselor when he heard a voice behind him.

"What's your hurry?"

"Leigh, I'm sorry. I didn't see you," he answered. He checked his watch.

"I'm a little bit angry with you, Sweetie. I thought we would have already made our plans for the summer. When I didn't hear from you, I just decided I would come over to see you. Not a very gentlemanly thing of you not to call. My parents have their beach place at St. Simon's and want to know when you can come. And you know, we have lots to talk about for next year. The Zetas are having their summer house party and you need to get the date on your calendar."

Jack took a breath. "Leigh, I'm sorry. Sorry about a lot of things. Sorry I didn't call like you expected. Sorry if I haven't been the gentleman that you deserve." He stepped away from the doorway for more privacy. "Something has happened. Something that changes things for us."

Leigh frowned. "What do you mean changes for us?" she hissed. "My parents are expecting you to come to St. Simon's. Our names are on the house party list!" Her voice grew louder.

Jack's parents had taught him well about manners and respect. He had never faced this kind of situation and had always been the one to do the right thing. He checked his watch again. "Leigh, I really need to get on the road. I wish there was a better way."

"A better way? A better way to break up with me?"

"Leigh, we had some dates. They were nice. But there's no way to break up something that never was."

"I see…" she all but yelled. "I'm not your sweet little Jessie. Jessie, who everyone adores. Poor, poor Jessie who lost her boyfriend in Vietnam."

"Wait! You can stop right there! Carter was a good friend and he gave his life for our country, Leigh. I'm not going to stand here and listen to you belittle my friends this way." He turned and walked away.

"Jack Mason!" she hollered, but he kept walking. It was almost as if a burden was lifted from his shoulders—a burden he hadn't even known he'd had.

THE GROUP SAT IN THE CHAPMAN farmhouse in complete silence, all processing the incredible sequence of events that had brought them all together. Then Stephen cleared his throat.

"We are so happy that you two decided to come today. And given your story, one never knows what life will bring us. I would have been disappointed if I had moved before you came to visit."

Everyone looked at Stephen, confusion on their faces. "Moved?" said Comfort.

"Yes," said Stephen. "I have spoken to the bishop. My sabbatical time has come to an end, and I've received my next assignment. I'm going to the chaplaincy at Fort Jackson in Columbia."

Matt straightened his shoulders and nodded. "Reverend, I guess it's time for us both to do what we're called to do." He placed his arm around his sister. "Starr, I know you had hoped for something different, but just like the reverend here, I have a new assignment." He looked around the room. "I've been called to return to Ft. Benning. I leave in a few days to rejoin the troops in Nam. I would appreciate all of your prayers."

Any doubts Stephen might have had about his new position as a military chaplain fell away. "Yes, you will have our prayers, Matt, and so will the soldiers with you. And you, too, Starr. I will pray for you and the hope you will bring to those on your concert tour."

Stephen placed his arm around Comfort. "And I will pray with gratitude for all your help in bringing Camp Greenwood to a reality."

He turned finally to Paul. "Prayers for you, my friend. I have faith that this is that chance for a change in life you so deserve."

Paul's eyes welled with tears as he listened to Stephen encourage the gathered group. "And we will pray for Stephen," he said. "Our prayers are with you as well and for those at Fort Jackson who will know the grace and hope you will provide."

IT HAD BEEN A TYPICAL CROSS Hill morning for Yates Bryan. Main Street was quiet, and the stores were yet to open. He could see a light on in the General and he slowed down to confirm all was well. He passed a house down the road where a man and his young son were loading up their hunting dog to head out to the fields beyond town.

He could see the joy of the father-son relationship. *Must be nice*, he thought. *Maybe I'll get back to some hunting one day.*

The cruiser seemed to have a mind of its own. Yates made a turn down the highway and ended up at the mailbox at the Chapman farm road. When he pulled into the driveway, Comfort went to the window to see who was approaching. "It's Sheriff Yates," he said.

Yates stepped from his cruiser and Stephen opened the door to welcome him. "Haven't seen you in a while, Sheriff. We have guests. I have a pot of coffee. Won't you join us?"

"Thanks. I'd love a cup," said Yates. He stepped through the doorway as the others stood to his arrival.

"I believe you know Starr and Matt," said Stephen.

Comfort eyed the sheriff and thought of how their mother Christine always seemed to avoid seeing him when she came to the farm.

Yates shook Matt's hand. "We don't ever seem to cross paths much. Nice to see you, Matt. And Starr. How's your mom?"

"She's fine," answered Starr. "Doing her best to keep up with our whereabouts. We flew up this morning from Atlanta."

"You flew?"

"Yep," said Matt. "A pilot's license comes in handy now and then. I don't get here much with my schedule."

Yates tried to maintain his composure. "Comfort keeps me informed about the family. I heard you did a tour in Vietnam. "

"Yes, sir," answered Matt.

Yates studied the young man. He was pleased with his respectful manners. Looking at him was almost like seeing his younger self in a mirror. He glanced at Starr. "You too, young lady. Last I heard, you were singing up and down the coast."

"She's making it big," said Comfort with pride. "Going on tour soon with a new song!"

Starr blushed. "I'm hoping for the best with it. We were just hearing from these guys about all our *unbelievable* connections."

Yates turned back to Matt. "What's next for you?"

"I'm going back to Nam for another tour," Matt answered. "I've got orders, and I'll be signing off on them soon." He looked at Starr and thought about Jessie. "Making other changes right now just isn't in the cards."

Starr looked at Yates. "I had hoped he would join me on tour."

Yates touched Matt's shoulder. "Well, we're all proud of your service. If you ever decide to make a change, we could use some good help here in the county. Always room for some new blood on the force here, especially with your kind of experience."

THE FLIGHT BACK TO ATLANTA WAS a quiet one for the two Randall siblings. Starr looked over at Matt several times and knew her brother well enough to know what was on his mind. When they touched down at the Peachtree-Dekalb Airport, she watched him sign out with the terminal manager and went to the car to wait. Once he was in the car, she started the engine and shifted into gear. "You were so quiet on our return," she said.

"Guess the word from the lieutenant on my orders has me preoccupied."

"Do you have to go back so soon?"

His answer was not what Starr expected. "Yes, but I was also thinking about Jessie. She told me how she feels about her friend Jack. The reverend and Mr. O'Conner knew Carter and Jessie well—and their hopes and dreams. I think Carter knew Jack would make sure Jessie would realize her hopes...just in a different way from me."

"So you're just going to give up on her?"

"It's not that I'm giving up. It's just I know what's in her heart. Besides, there's something bigger here than both of us—a greater cause. I have come to see that. A head and heart thing, you know. The farm and just flying above it all helped me see that in many ways."

"Is this about Dad? Is this all his doing?"

"That's part of it. Maybe. But who knows, maybe down the road what Sheriff Bryan said might be a possibility."

"Giving up the military for law enforcement? In Cross Hill?" she asked.

"You know, Sis, when he looked at me and told me he was proud of my service...I can't explain it, but it was like he really knew me."

Chapter 34

J essie left the bank with her father and sat in the car without a word. She'd given the bank officer the first royalty check and signed all the final foundation papers.

"What made you decide to do this?" asked her father.

Jessie smiled. "So much has come together in the last few weeks, Dad. The reverend's call to you about looking for help for the Cross Hill community and then when Coach O'Connor called and told me about the camp—I kept hearing Mr. Baker's words about doing for others. It just became clear."

She reached in her purse for the medallion from Carter. "One day at a time," said her father when he saw it. "It's a beautiful message from Carter for us all. And a foundation to honor him is a wonderful idea. So where do you go from here?"

"I'll let Coach know I am good for helping with the camp this summer. My time at Egleston has given me a lot of ideas about how to help those children in South Carolina." She looked at her dad. "The decision we've made at the bank should remain between you, Mom and me. I don't want them to know I have anything to do with it."

Ladd nodded. "Your mom and I will make sure all goes well while you're at the camp this summer."

"I will leave right after Claire and Tom's wedding."

On the way home, she thought about Matt and how best to share the news of her leaving.

JESSIE PULLED INTO A SPACE AT the park and looked down at the basket on the car seat next to her. She thought of how sacred the park had become to her. In her mind's eye, she saw Carter playing pickup football games and sitting with her on the Peachtree Creek bank. She saw Jack's face when Carter asked him to watch out for her. She heard the whispers in her heart that had told her to embrace Jack's love on her walk there.

Matt had played a special part in the weeks they had come to know each other. His letter had planted the seeds of acceptance for Carter's decision and gratitude for any young man's dedication of military service. Their Cross Hill flight through the skies of peace and trust had brought her the courage she needed to bring joy to her life and the lives of others. She wanted to share all that with him even with the knowledge they would go their separate ways.

"Wow," said Matt when he stepped from his car and saw her lift the basket from her car.

Jessie smiled. "You didn't know about the fine dining here, did you?"

"No, I didn't," replied Matt. "Five-star, I'm sure." He smiled and took the basket from her hand. She reached in the back seat for a quilt.

"Over there," she pointed. "There's an oak near the creek bank."

They spread the quilt and sat down. Matt watched as Jessie lifted the containers of food from the basket. Both displayed little appetite—they sat quietly and nibbled while watching the rushing waters of the creek. Neither wanted to begin what they both knew was an inevitable conversation.

Jessie looked up. "I wanted to come here with you because it has been my special place in so many ways. It was important to me that you saw it."

"Is this the place? The one you told me about after you received my letter?"

Jessie nodded. "I know it doesn't seem like much, but it is sacred to me." Jessie looked out over the creek. "That camp you heard about when you went with Starr to Cross Hill? Coach O'Connor has called and asked me to work there this summer."

Matt smiled. "That's great, Jessie. They will be lucky to have you. I am glad you will experience the special place that is important to me... just like this one." He touched her hand and looked first into her eyes, then away.

Lt. Thacker's words to him months ago drifted into his mind. *Your own feelings will be matched by the pain and grief of their loved ones. It can tear you apart just as much, even more. But it can be a gift to them too. Closure they may be searching for.*

Jessie waited for him to turn back to her. "You've made your decision, haven't you?" she said. "You're going back to Vietnam."

After a brief hesitation, Matt nodded. "As much as I envisioned something else, I think you and I both knew this day would come from the beginning."

Jessie reached to embrace Matt. "You have made a difference in my life, Matt. I can never thank you enough."

"Just be happy, Jess. That will be thanks enough." He held her tightly and wiped a tear from her cheek. "You can do me a favor, though."

"Anything," said Jessie.

"Be a friend to Starr," he said. "The two of you have a lot to offer." Matt thought of the danger inherent in the assignment he had accepted. "I know you both will look out for each other and do great things."

PAUL AND STEPHEN MET ELIZABETH AT the camp office to go over more details about the plans for summer. Abbott was hanging up the phone when they arrived at his office. He shook his head and stood to greet them. "I can't believe it!"

"What?" said Elizabeth. "Is it bad news about our permits for the camp?"

"No," said Abbott, shaking his head. "It's great news! That was a bank in Atlanta. An anonymous benefactor will cover all our expenses for the camp. Everything we will need."

Paul looked at Stephen. "The best way to predict the future is to create it," Stephen said. The others in the room looked at him and he continued. "That's a quote from a plaque at the Chapman farm. The future here has been blessed. We are being given all the tools to create something very special. Ours is not to ask how or why but to be the best stewards of the opportunity before us."

"You're right," said Paul. "We were all brought together for a purpose." He looked over at Elizabeth and smiled.

JESSIE WATCHED AS MATT PULLED AWAY from the park and said a silent prayer that he would be safe. She started her car and headed down Longwood toward home. When she turned into the driveway, she saw a Volkswagen parked in front of the house, and her parents in conversation with its owner on the steps. She slammed on the brakes and jumped out of her car, running toward the trio, and was met by Jack who threw his arms around her. "Jessie, I didn't see your letter until today!" He lifted her off the ground. "I didn't know! I didn't know."

She looked into his eyes with tears of happiness. "You're here now. That's all that matters."

WHEN MATT OPENED THE DOOR TO the apartment, his phone was ringing. He picked it up to hear Lt. Thacker say, "Randall, it's time. We ship out day after tomorrow at 0600."

Resolute, he returned the receiver to its base and looked around the apartment. Starr would keep it as her base in Atlanta for times when she met with Perry or sang in the area. He glanced at the lengthy performance list on the counter—"The Hope Tour."

His duffel was almost full—one last item, Jessie's letter, was left to place on top. It would be his good luck charm going forward. He thought about their final embrace and made his way to his car for an early morning drive across town.

There was one other thing to do before leaving.

Chapter 35

Madeline moved around the dressing room, helping the girls in Claire's bridal party. She zipped the back of Jessie's dress and gave her daughter a hug.

The wedding coordinator passed out floral bouquets so one last photo could be taken before the ceremony. As she handed Jessie's to her, she whispered. "Claire told me to tell you that *your* bouquet is special." Jessie looked down to see a red rose tucked at the base of the other white and pink roses.

Claire moved beside her. "It's just a remembrance from someone I know who wants you to be happy today," she said. "Tom and I want to thank you for teaching us to keep hope in our hearts and to always take…" She paused. "One day at a time."

The bride and bridesmaids smiled for the photographer and moved to get into position as they'd practiced the evening before. Tom was nervous and his groomsmen provided the lightheartedness needed as the countdown was heard.

The minister gathered the men for a final word of encouragement. Tom looked to his father. "You have the ring?" His father nodded and patted the inside pocket of his tuxedo. Then he stepped forward and gave his son a hug.

The sounds of the organ and a violin began. In place for the processional, Jessie looked up ahead at the groomsmen and smiled with joy for the wedding day of her friends. So did the groomsman first in line to process down the aisle toward the altar. Jessie glanced down at the red rose in her bouquet and breathed a prayer for the event that had brought everyone to this day.

The minister's words and the vows exchanged embraced the spirit among those present—those who knew not only the joy of the wedding couple but also the life's sorrows of their friends and family. "Till death us do part," the couple repeated.

The official marriage announcement brought Tom and Claire's awaited kiss and the organ played. Claire reached for her bouquet to walk up the aisle with her new husband. She turned to Jessie and smiled acknowledging all they had shared.

Jessie waited her turn and then walked to the center to take the arm of her assigned groomsman. Jack's hand was there even before she reached him. As they took their first steps out of the church, he leaned in to whisper, "You look beautiful," he said. "All packed?"

Jessie wrapped her arm around his and whispered, "I am."

THE SATURDAY MORNING SKIES WERE PEACEFUL and bright blue—not a cloud in the sky. It had been a several days since Matt's visit with Starr to the farm. The Peachtree-DeKalb Airport attendant saluted him upon his morning arrival at the tarmac gate.

The exhilaration of his takeoff confirmed the importance of his decision—to experience one last glimpse of the peace that would elude him in the days to come.

The countryside smiled up at him as Matt followed his course to the South Carolina Upstate. Soon he saw the farmland that had embraced him since childhood. Friends at the campground below recognized his low-flying altitude and waved their hats and scarves. Matt dipped the wings of the plane to acknowledge them and made a final circle.

Stephen's books and cherished communion set were carefully packed and his bags were in the trunk of his car. He walked down to the lake, whistling to the horses that joined him along the fences. The lake waters gleamed. When he saw the plane circle the farmhouse and back toward the family cemetery, he held his hand high and waved.

Paul O'Connor, the new occupant of the Chapman farmhouse was busy preparing for his Camp Greenwood counselors and staff. He smiled at the thought of how Elizabeth had brought him some of the homemade breads and jams from The Mercantile and vegetables from Spencer Adams's farm stand. The gesture gave him a good excuse to invite her to dinner soon.

He stepped out onto the porch for another sip of coffee. A sound in the sky disturbed the usual quiet of the morning. He raised his hand above his brow and squinted toward the southwest.

Comfort stood up from his early work in the rose garden and shielded his eyes from the sun. He dropped his clippers and waved his arms. "Brave journey, Mr. Matt," he whispered.

Yates Bryan stopped his patrol car on the Cross Hill highway and looked to the sky at the small plane heading back south. He thought of Christine and the future of the young man flying toward an unknown future.

Abbott Charles leaned back in his office chair. The coffee pot sat ready to fill the cups of volunteers making their way to the camp. He looked out the window to see the first group of volunteers arriving.

Elizabeth and Jeb led the way in their pickup truck loaded with supplies and pulling a horse trailer transporting some of their horses from the Chapman farm. When they arrived, he watched the brother and sister, with their endless energy, rally the team of volunteers circled around them for their assignments.

The mail on Abbott's desk lay waiting for his attention and the envelope postmarked Atlanta was soon discovered. A golden seal with a red rose as its emblem and the words "Hope Foundation" was embossed below it in the upper corner. His eyes grew big when he opened the letter to find its contents.

STARR STOOD ON THE BALCONY OF the apartment, still overwhelmed by the events since her trip to Nashville. Rehearsals with new band mates had been arranged in studios near Perry's office—she'd sat in on tryouts by over twenty-five singers vying to be part of her backup band. A stage crew still needed to be hired and she had appointments to schedule with the costume designers and hair and makeup teams who would travel with her on the road.

She had released her dream of Matt's giving up his military career and joining her on the road, but his decision to return to Vietnam had come too soon. Their mother's earlier call of encouragement meant the world to her, but when Matt had driven away, she couldn't dismiss the feeling of being alone again.

She picked up her faithful Gibson and sat on the sofa. "Old girl, I guess it is just you and me now," she said. She strummed the chords of

Hope, which had become a sort of prayer for her. Tears flowed down her cheeks. *"Tomorrow wishes you next to me,"* she sang. *"Hope and love that gift to see...."*

A loud knock at the door interrupted her singing and she frowned. She hadn't had time to meet any of her neighbors. "Just a minute!" she called. Still holding her guitar, she stepped to the door and opened it.

A young man from Nashville stood wearing a Stetson and holding a bouquet of flowers. He brought another Stetson from behind his back—a red one with "Starr" in rhinestones on the brim.

"I can't believe you're here!" she exclaimed.

"Well, you *said* if I was ever in Atlanta to look you up."

Chapter 36

Acouple of hours after the wedding reception ended, Jack pulled into the driveway of Jessie's Longwood home. Jessie appeared on the steps wearing his Northwest football jersey and carrying the quilt he had given her at the shoals. She hurried to the car, handed her suitcase to him, and hopped into the car.

As they pulled out of the driveway, Jessie and Jack lowered their windows and waved. Ladd and Madeline stood arm in arm and watched their daughter drive away, filled with a newfound joy.

Jessie took a deep breath and imagined the adventures waiting ahead for them. At the corner, Jack turned the Volkswagen and headed for the highway toward South Carolina. He shifted gears and looked over at Jessie. "Are you ready for this?"

Jessie felt the whisper of a breeze across her face. She reached for the hand that had always been there for her and said, with all her heart…

"Ready!"

My gratitude for the journey ...

THE PAST YEARS HAVE BROUGHT MANY challenges for us all, and some were very unexpected. At the time of the release of *A Heart's Memory* in late 2020, I received a breast cancer diagnosis that brought my life into full perspective. *After All* had one meaning when I began this sequel and another when we received the pathology report. Through it all, I found an inner peace with the thoughts, prayers, encouragement and support of my family, friends, and professionals.

My thanks goes out to the many, many medical professionals and staff who brought me through it all and to the day when I received my *after all* clear mammogram followup in the summer of 2021. My journal entries during the journey are many and I celebrate and say a special thank you to my team of physicians, healthcare and well-being professionals.

- Dr. David Schammel, MD, Susan Webb, BSN, OCN
- Dr. Steven Allgood, MD, Dr. Joe Stephenson, MD, Dr. Michael Zurenko, MD
- The Cancer Center Radiation Team: Heather, Crissy, Trish, Teresa
- Dr. Chyrel Stoner, MD and Dr. Patricia Crawford, MD
- Angela Breazeale, LMT and Alecia Moreau, LE, CYT

While others are experiencing grief, health, family and world challenges, I send you a *peace that surpasses all understanding. M*y hope, faith and encouragement for you is to *take one day at a time.* Brave journey, my friends.

After all … sharing hope with one another is the ultimate gift.

Acknowledgments

As the years have passed and the writing began, I cannot begin to express all the love and gratitude to so many individuals who have touched my life. Family has sustained me through the days and years of celebrations and challenging ups and downs, joys and sadness. Some individuals are no longer with us and others have been and continue to be my inspiration from early childhood to high school, college and beyond.

My Northside High and other school and church friends, ministers, teachers, and coaches played a major role in speaking to my heart. It led me to this calling to put into words the experiences shared in *A Heart's Memory* and its sequel even until today. Gratitude is the heart's memory to Babs, Barbara, Carol, Crow, Diane, Eddie, Elaine, Gary, Harry, Jack, Melissa, Nancy, Peggy, Phyllis, Sherry and so many more.

College and sorority life friendships continue to influence the thoughts of days gone by and how much it played a role in *After All*. Angela, Cecilia, Em, Linda, Dale, Kay, Mary Beth, Ruth, Sandra, Susan and more played a role in helping me see that life's journey will forever be cherished for the joy of those days at UGA.

To my editor, Vally Sharpe: Thank you for your guidance and perfection to bring Jessie and Jack's story to this point and helping me to share more than words with my readers so that they will know that hope is always there for them.

I am proud to celebrate once again the artistic gifts of my granddaughter Leira Johnson for her cover art. It is of great joy for me that my grandson, Jay Israel, and Chelsea Marks posed for Leira's sketching for the cover.

The journey will continue in the days to follow for this love story and life ahead for Coach, Comfort, Christine, Elizabeth, Matt, Sam, Starr and Yates.

About the Author

JANICE R. JOHNSON was born and raised in Atlanta, Georgia. For many years she taught business classes on the community college level until called to become a church administrator, a career that would last over thirty years, and for which she would receive national honors, including induction into the Church Management Hall of Fame at the time of her retirement.

In 2004, she co-authored a book with Ruben Swint, *Weaving our Lives Together*. Janice and her husband John live in Greenville, S.C., and have two children and six grandchildren.

After All is Janice's second novel, a sequel to *A Heart's Memory*, which was published in 2021. A third book is planned to complete the trilogy.